Sliver of Evil

by

D J Walker

Book One of the Tek & Nika Series

D J Walker
P.O. Box 145
Sloansville, NY 12160
U.S.A.

paperback ISBN: 979-8-9874553-0-2
ebook ISBN: 979-8-9874553-1-9

December 2022

Tek & Nika Series ~ speaking of shapeshifters ~
Book 1 – Sliver Of Evil
Book 2 – Nika Rising
Book 3 – Sinuous Passages

Chapter 1

(The time — prehistoric. The place — the northeastern forests of what is now the United States of America.)

Tek and his older brother Sho were born into one of the smaller settlements of the People. In a clearing scraped from the endless forest, they lived far from the larger, more powerful knats that thrived along the great river and the main pathways through the forest.

Their small knat was peaceable, but fearless when a fight could not be avoided. The other knats regarded it as a wolf regards a badger: anything that fought back so ferociously with tooth and claw was best left unmolested.

But though the knat staved off marauding by other knats, it could not forestall more elemental disasters.

When Tek and Sho were still children their knat was destroyed one broiling hot day by the panther wind's daughter.

Her name has been lost to time — even whispering it might, in an unlucky moment, draw her unwanted attention.

She lived in the deepest of the cold dark caves pocking the boglands, nursing her implacable hatred for all living things. As long as nothing disturbed her cave's dark chill, she tolerated the teeming infestation that habited above her in the life–giving light and warmth.

But on that sultry afternoon, the heat baking the earth's crust forced long greasy ripples of warmth into the still air of her cave, shattering the perfection of her chasmal retreat.

Panther wind's daughter knew who to blame for the unholy disturbance: *Them* in the Sky World had let their great fire blaze too hot. If only *They* had bestirred themselves to tamp it down, she might have borne the misery, though grumblingly. But no, the disturbance in her cave worsened, until the sullied chill could not soothe her, nor contain her fury.

1

Up she surged; in a violent rush she burst from the cave through fissures. Blinded by light and oppressed by unrelieved heat, she gathered her strength and fought her way upward, into the sky.

She eddied there, in heavy air well above the treetops, bent on destruction. *Them* of the high up Sky World were too far beyond wind's highest reach, but all below her was vulnerable. Everything clinging to earth's crust — the tangled verdure and the creatures crawling through it — was within her ire's reach.

She slipped in behind her father as he loped through the sizzling hot sky. Despite the oppressive heat his chuffing breath sent heavy flutters of breeze down through earth's growth. She followed him, winking in and out of whorls cascading from his hot breath, as they fell in broad spirals, off and away from the massive panther pelt slung across his shoulders.

As panther wind passed over the hapless knat where Tek and Sho lived, his daughter conjured her great pot. Planting her feet on the crags of distant mountaintops, she muttered sacred words that thundered across the sky — words that forced her father's spent breath to arc around to her in a great rushing circle.

Too late he discovered the theft of his spent breath. Stilled until his daughter's fury was spent, he hovered high in the sky while she swept his winds down, down into her capacious pot.

She stirred his stolen breath round and around, faster — ever faster. She infused it with her own manic breath, until the unwieldy amalgam roared in her pot with an unstoppable violence. And when the maelstrom reached its thrumming height, she seized her pot and upended it, slinging its contents in a great swath across earth's trembly surface.

The knat's clearing could not have been more directly in the path of the pot's heedless, savage winds. Everything was instantly and violently ripped apart. The plantings in the carefully–tended fields — snapped and flattened. The tall, heavy logs of the knat walls — scattered like chaff. And the long sturdy clanhouses of log and bark — flung apart as if mere leaf litter. Many of the knaters died or were mortally wounded instantly — crushed and strewn about like flailing beetles cascading from a falling, rotted log.

Sho and Tek's parents and their closer relatives were among the many who died that day, in the blind fury of the panther wind's daughter.

*   *   *

Along with the rest of the knat's living remnants Sho and Tek gathered and mourned their dead.

Having decided to stay independent of the other knats, the beleaguered knat hastily built shelters in a new place, and gathered what it would need for survival through winter.

Sho and Tek could have left the knat and sought a home for themselves among distant relatives in another knat, depending on clan sufferance for their admission. But they stayed with the knat of their birth, to add their efforts to its desperate fight for survival.

Fortunately, that winter's bear wind did not beset the land as harshly as usual. He did not pass through the frozen forest as often, with his midnight black fur matted and hoary with his frozen breath.

When the fawn warmth at length returned to the world, the knaters established new planting fields and built sturdy new clanhouses inside a fine new circular knat wall. Though they made ample allowance for future growth, the wall's circumference was diminished, as were the lengths of the new clanhouses. It would be several lifetimes before the knat grew to its former size.

Because the knat had decided against combining with another knat, it would have to grow mainly through the childbearing of its fecund women.

A woman of the People always stayed with the clanhouse and knat of her birth. When she married, her husband could be a man from the knat she belonged to, or he could be a man from another knat who was willing to leave his knat and join hers upon their marriage. Though either way, he could not be too closely related to her by clan.

Whenever there were more available women than men, the knat worked to persuade men from other knats to marry into their knat. When, instead, there were more available men than women, the superfluous men had to choose between staying without marrying, and leaving to marry into another knat.

The latter was the choice that Sho faced, some five years after the terrible losses caused by the panther wind's daughter. By then he had left childhood behind and wanted to marry, but there was a dearth of available women in the knat. His best chance for marrying would be to find a bride in another knat.

From a young age Sho had been like an adult in miniature — sturdy with a grave stare, steadily growing into his role as a prime provider and protector of his knat. For many years before becoming a man, he routinely went on the longer hunts with the men, having earned his place among them with his energy and strength, and with his stamina and avid attention to every detail of the hunting ways.

On these hunts they sometimes happened upon hunters from the large Ochwah knat. Since the two knats were usually on friendly terms they would then hunt together, sharing out the meat and hides of the kills. Thus the Ochwah hunters got to know Sho, and saw that he had the makings of an exceptionally good hunter.

When the Ochwah hunters found out that Sho was looking outside of his own knat for a bride, they invited him to visit their knat. Over the course of several visits, some of the clan mothers judged that he would make a good husband for one of their daughters or granddaughters. Before long clan mother S'Kaw and her granddaughter Tsihi came to terms with Sho, for Tsihi and Sho to marry the following spring.

When Sho married Tsihi he would leave his own knat and join the S'Kaw clanhouse in the Ochwah knat. Since this would leave his younger brother Tek with no close family in the knat of their birth, Sho asked clan mother S'Kaw if Tek could come with him and join her clanhouse as well.

Sho's request was understandable, but it was unusual. S'Kaw insisted on meeting Tek before deciding. Very early in the spring of Tek's fourteenth year, Sho took him to the Ochwah knat.

Tek was eager to stay with his brother Sho after his marriage, so he wanted to be accepted into the Ochwah knat. He did not think he would ever be as important a hunter and warrior as his older brother, but he believed that he could become a valued member of the knat.

He was lighter in build than Sho, and lacked his brother's inborn confidence. His nature was more reflective and questioning. He whole–heartedly embraced his duty to become a skilled hunter and warrior, but he was diffident about how he would meet its more arduous requirements. His arrows when he hunted small game did not seem to fly as swift and true as his older brother's had at the same age, and the fish in the streams seemed more resistant to his bone hooks and scap nets, than they had been to Sho's. Lacking Sho's heavier set, he had to depend on an eel–like slipperiness in a fight. This was less respected than brute strength, but Tek was not ashamed of it. He could not help what he had been born with, and what he had been born without.

He would make the most of what he had. And surely, he felt, given some time he would show this clan mother S'Kaw that he was willing to work very hard to earn his place in her clanhouse.

The S'Kaw clanhouse was one of the furthest from the narrow, curving entrance way in the high wall encircling the Ochwah knat. As Sho led Tek to it, some of the knaters silently watched them pass. A few of the older boys began to follow them. Sho and Tek went directly to their destination, without stopping to speak with anyone. They were in their best clothes. Sho walked naturally, with dignity; Tek tried to walk with the same bearing as his brother.

Someone must have alerted S'Kaw that they were coming. She stood at the main door on the east end of her clanhouse, a bony old woman with dark, deep–set eyes. When the brothers reached her, she swept the hide door aside and motioned Sho inside, telling him that he should go and talk with Tsihi. As the hide door flapped back into place, S'Kaw stared fixedly at Tek. He tried to meet her gaze calmly.

Suddenly S'Kaw punched his chest with both fists, knocking the breath out of him. She was a strong old woman: her punch was like being hit with a rock. It caught Tek off balance. He fell backward and tumbled sideways onto the muddy ground.

He scrambled to get up but S'Kaw shoved him back down. She beat him away from her clanhouse, and toward a rank muddy pit.

If his attacker had been a man or a boy, Tek would have grappled him down into the mud. If his attacker had been any *other* woman than this one, he would have tripped her up and shoved back until *she* was the one tipped into the muddy pit. But he could not fight back against this clan mother, no matter what caused her to beat him away from her clanhouse. Whether she was insane, or was testing him . . .

Tek measured the rhythm of S'Kaw's blows, and at just the right moment he sprung back from her, blocking her flailing arms enough to keep himself just beyond her reach. He saved himself from sliding into the pit by dropping and clawing himself away from it. S'Kaw skirted the pit and lunged toward him again and again but he wove and dodged, blunting most of her blows.

Watching each other carefully S'Kaw and Tek went through several more rapid lunges and feints. S'Kaw flapped her arms, making herself seem larger, and she always kept herself between Tek and her clanhouse, while Tek strove to stay close to her clanhouse but beyond her reach. He was strongly reminded of a big gawky turkey buzzard defending its log nest against an intruder. Turkey buzzards were ungainly–looking birds, but they could be surprisingly fast and powerful in a ground attack. Tek tried to look back at S'Kaw with a calm, haughty face, despite being smeared with filth and feeling deeply wronged. S'Kaw had the right to reject him, but if she did then he wanted to be able to leave this knat with as much dignity as he could manage.

As their grim 'dance' continued Tek thought he could see flickers of something in S'Kaw's eyes, that he had not thought possible after her initial attack. He thought he could see . . . some slight, grudging approval.

With a leap of intuition and the agility of his youth Tek shot past S'Kaw, enduring her blows as he passed her. He planted himself before the door of her clanhouse. "Grandmother," he said quickly, "I pledge myself to keep your clanhouse safe." His voice was not as deep and even as he would have liked, but he spoke as clearly and firmly as his ragged breath permitted.

S'Kaw rushed up but she did not flail at him. She went face to face, so close that Tek could smell the spring onion in her sweat. While he looked back as calmly as possible, she minutely examined every pore and hair of his face, and then her gaze lingered on his eyes. He did not know what he read in them. All he got were fleeting glimpses of her impenetrable calculations and measurings of his worth to her clanhouse. And then just for an instant, he thought he saw an odd little flicker, as if something she saw surprised or confounded her.

S'Kaw backed off slightly and laughed at him. But it was the laugh of an irritated elder, rather than that of a mortal enemy. Tek breathed a little more evenly and hazarded a quick glance around.

Quite a number of the knaters had gathered to watch, all at a distance and all silent except for some low murmurings here and there. But the only one that Tek looked for was his brother Sho. There was a young woman by Sho's side, who could only be Tsihi, his brother's intended bride. They were both looking on with expressions of great surprise and concern. Tsihi in particular — her large dark eyes were full open and round, her head jerked a little, sideways and back, as her small mouth fluttered open and shut.

Their surprise reassured Tek more than anything else that had happened since he had arrived at the knat, because it meant that S'Kaw's attack was not at all typical of her. He reasoned that her attack had *not* sprung from an instability, or a strange, hardened malice. He began to hope that he might be accepted into this clanhouse after all.

He watched S'Kaw very carefully though. She was still very much in striking range.

S'Kaw finished having her laugh and told Tek offhandedly to go wash himself off in the river. Then, she ordered, he was to come inside and dry himself by the fire. She shoved him away as she walked past him into the clanhouse, but it was a casual shove.

Tek's finery was spoiled, but S'Kaw had accepted him.

It was decided. When Sho married Tsihi, both brothers were to move into the S'Kaw clanhouse of the Ochwah knat.

7

Chapter 2

Sho and Tek arrived late in the day, on the day before the wedding, bringing all of their belongings. They carried their weapons in their hands. Clothes and small tools were rolled tightly into skins that they carried on their backs.

Until the wedding on the evening of the next day, Sho and Tek stayed as guests in one of the clanhouses next to S'Kaw's. Sho had timed their arrival so they would only have to spend the night and part of the next day in the clanhouse. Tek soon understood why. As soon as they arrived, the men of the clanhouse began giving Sho copious advice about marriage, interspersed with nearly incomprehensible jokes that they thought were extremely funny.

They were enjoying being surrogate fathers and uncles. Sho endured their advice and strange ribbing with a tight smile, not wishing to give offense. But Tek could see that it was often an ordeal for his proud, self–reliant older brother.

On the morning of the wedding an older boy of the clanhouse was told to show Tek around. While he did so, he warned Tek about Okat.

Above all else, Tek should avoid the woman Okat. That would be easy to do, the boy said, because she lived on the other side of the knat, in a clanhouse near the entranceway in the knat's wall. The knat was big enough that boys on their side of the knat rarely were in direct contact with the women of the clanhouses on the other side.

Unlike the men who were vexing Sho with their copious advice and jokes, the boy kept his warning about Okat to a minimum. Afterward he took Tek on a roundabout route to where the women were preparing a clearing for the spring planting of maize. From a distance and hidden by some bushes that were already leafing out, the boy pointed Okat out to Tek.

From that distance Okat looked much like the others, except Tek noticed that while the others were working in small clusters, Okat worked alone. She also seemed to be working much more slowly than the others — in fact, hardly at all.

Tek wasn't sure if he would recognize Okat at close range, but by that night he knew exactly who she was.

Early in the evening the entire knat gathered near the center of the knat for the wedding ceremony, beside the big fire pit. The fire was lit and Sho and Tsihi were married, along with three other couples.

As a newcomer Tek stayed in the background during the ceremony and the feast, helping along with the other boys his age when asked to bring more firewood, or to fetch reed mats or skins. At the feast after the wedding he ate his fill, and then wandered through the shifting clusters of knaters, watching and listening idly. The light was fading. Soon after dark the chanting and dancing would begin. He made himself as inconspicuous as possible, feeling like a silent animal of the forest coming a little closer to the People to observe their smells, their sounds and their ways, while they were distracted by the strictures of their rituals.

In his new surroundings, and because of the importance of the ceremony he had just witnessed, Tek felt more attune with the spiritual ways than usual. At moments he even imagined that some of the knaters emitted the scents of various forest creatures, and had some of their mannerisms. A few of those of S'Kaw's clanhouse had the dryly pungent scent of birds of prey, and they were wont to bounce on their feet, or flutter their hands and arms, when speaking excitedly to their neighbors. A few others, that Tek later learned were from clanhouses on the other side of the knat, had more of the musky scent of the forest's larger furred animals. Their bodies were bulkier, and their movements slower, more confident and deliberate than those of the other knaters. It also seemed to Tek that their low voices sometimes sounded like the growls and grunts of those animals.

Tek found himself near two women of this latter group. As he caught their oddly strong bear scent on the breeze and listened to the growly cadence of their low murmurings, he watched them without seeming to. They were sitting, leaning toward each other. He could

9

not hear what they were saying but the older one, who was stout and had a rounded curve to her shoulders and back, seemed to be speaking bluntly and firmly to the younger one. The younger one, who was taller and thinner but with the same rounded curves, apparently did not like what the older one was saying. She rolled herself back and forth, and then sprang up impatiently. Rapidly she strode over to a group of women who were talking and laughing among themselves.

As soon as the women realized that the bear–like woman had joined them, they all fell silent and their faces expressed dismay and wariness. Immediately Tek thought that the woman who had joined the group might be Okat — the woman he had been told to avoid. He scanned the rest of the crowd and saw the boy who had warned him about Okat that morning. The boy was also watching the group of women; he glanced at Tek, nodded slowly, and gave Tek the hunter's sign to keep still and to keep back. Now Tek was certain that the woman who had joined the group was Okat. He watched the group with more interest.

Okat had singled out a young woman in the group and was berating her. Her words were difficult for Tek to hear but he caught the words 'husband' and 'thief' in Okat's battering, bullying tirade. The young woman was small and slight. She backed away a few steps and her body seemed to wilt under Okat's onslaught of words. Even so, Tek noticed a brightness in her eyes that belied a complete submission to the tirade.

This vestige of impudence seemed to enrage Okat. Her taunts became angrier and louder. Nearby knaters quieted, listening, and Tek clearly heard Okat ordering the young woman to stay away from her husband, in a torrent of brutal, vicious insults and threats. To reinforce her furious words Okat advanced on the young woman, but instead of backing further away the slight, younger woman stood her ground, fidgeting in an odd way. Her eyes flashed with a cooler anger than Okat's, and contained a warning of her own toward Okat that Tek could not interpret. But it seemed ludicrous to him that the smaller woman — who was hardly more than a girl and had not spoken a word back to Okat — could be any match for Okat.

Before the two women could clash the other women in the group stepped in between them to separate them. At first their words and movements were hesitant, but they quickly reinforced each other. In moments the women were scuffling with Okat, in a tight, determined knot around her — while the young woman was edged out of the group by two older woman and pulled further away and out of sight.

The women around Okat uttered sharp exclamations as Okat swiped and spit and roared at them, but they pushed and hit back. Okat had started this fight; they would not let her win it so easily, not against them all.

Other knaters began to murmur that this fighting should stop — a wedding feast was no place for a quarrel like this.

The stout older woman, who had been speaking to Okat before she accosted the young woman, got up and lumbered over to the scuffle. As soon as she stood up Tek could see that she wore the ceremonial robes of a clan mother. She forced her way into the circle around Okat and disappeared. Then abruptly the circle expanded as the women stepped back from the center. The noise quieted and the older woman could be heard speaking as Okat stood glowering beside her.

"And just what did you expect from my poor daughter, at such a time as this, when so many couples are being newly joined? Could you expect her to be silent about the harm that someone has been doing to her own joining, made many springs ago now? Can you expect her to let someone of another clanhouse take something away from her, that still belongs to her?"

She continued to speak in this vein. Superficially her gruff voice had a wheedling, reasoning tone, but there was no mistaking that she expected to be deferred to. After all she was a clan mother, besides being Okat's mother. Tek later learned that her name was S'Och.

Most of the women in the group around S'Och and Okat looked like they did not agree with S'Och, but they made no response. One after another they dropped their angry eyes. Now that Okat's mother was putting her strength in with Okat's, it would be futile to battle against them both.

Another clan mother came up. She quietly but firmly told the women in the circle around S'Och and Okat to come help her in her clanhouse. They all complied, but as they left Okat smirked and taunted them in an undertone. They pretended to ignore her, but Tek saw a few of them flinch as if struck by a blow. They all looked

11

uneasy and defeated, even though it seemed to Tek that the scuffle had ended in a draw.

The boy who had warned Tek about Okat came over and stood beside Tek during the fracas. Now he spoke to Tek quietly. "Each one of them knows that Okat will get back at them, with something vicious. None of them will escape it."

"Especially the one that Okat was yelling at?" Tek asked, even though he thought he knew the answer.

The boy was silent for so long that Tek thought he wasn't going to bother to reply. But then the boy spoke.

"It is known in this knat that when Okat was just a girl, she and another girl teased each other a lot, and then they'd fight about it and about other things, always like two rough little kit panthers. Then they got a little older, and the other girl just wasn't very smart, because she couldn't see that Okat was getting more dangerous. She kept on fighting with her just like before.

"Then one day the two girls went out together to pick berries, but only Okat came back.

"Okat told everyone that the other girl just wandered away, and that she didn't know where she went. Many in the knat went out to look for her, including of course the hunters. But she was never found."

The boy stopped talking, but Tek sensed he had more to say. He waited, while they both watched some of the men ready themselves to make the music for the dancing. The men settled into a group upwind and a little to one side of the fire in the pit, arranging themselves with their drums and rattles. It was full dark now and the big fire at the center of the knat was throwing up the shadows of the knaters who were milling around.

The boy continued. "The one that you saw Okat yelling at, she is just barely a woman. Her name is Ani. She . . . hasn't been very smart. She has let Okat's husband Roh sleep with her.

"This is the third spring that Okat and Roh have been married, but there is still no child from Okat. Roh doesn't know whether it is because of him, or because of Okat. So he's been trying to find out, with Ani.

"It is very foolish of him and Ani, because it can't end well for either of them, now that Okat knows about what they are doing. Ani

12

will get the worst of it, unless her family guards her carefully from now on. Because if they don't, Okat will get to Ani, and if she does then I expect that Okat will kill her."

The boy spoke with conviction, but Tek knew that a knat would never condone a killing in a women's fight over a man. If Okat killed Ani, she would be banished from the knat, and that would mean death for her too, from exposure. "Surely Okat would not risk —"

"Oh, Okat will be clever. Maybe, something like the little girl who went berry picking with her and did not come back."

The chanting and dancing began then; the two boys went their separate ways. Tek was unsettled by the women's fight, and by what the boy had just told him. But it was time to put that aside, and become a part of the dancing.

He wasn't much of a dancer himself, though the drumming sometimes made his feet bounce lightly on the ground, and the chanting seemed like an eerie call from the forest, insisting that he leap and prance around the fire, with sinewy turns and fancy struts. He remembered dancing like that when he was a young child. His knat had pointedly laughed at his 'fancy dancing'. Thus he learned to keep to the proper steps and movements instead.

Each knat had its own version of the chanting and dancing traditions. It would take some time for Tek to learn the Ochwah knat's variants; in the meantime, he would watch the others to learn the main moves, and try to dance competently.

Tek wasn't even sure whether he should keep with the people he was staying with, or be in with the people of S'Kaw's clanhouse. The two groups were next to each other in the circle around the fire, so Tek chose a place between them. Soon the people of S'Kaw's clanhouse edged him further into their group, and he understood that he belonged with them now.

The first dances were slow group dances and Tek easily copied the steps as the dancers moved in a great westerly circle around the fire. The slow pace gave Tek plenty of time to look around the circle at the groups of dancers from the other clanhouses. Not too far ahead of the S'Kaw group he recognized the women who had encircled Okat during the fight; he even glimpsed Ani, small and light, dancing among those women. Further on and nearly across the circle from Tek, he recognized Okat and S'Och dancing with the others of their clanhouse.

For the most part the dancing was continuous; when the next dance began the music and chanting simply changed.

A faster dance began and the chanting and music for it had an urgency. Tek knew enough to understand that this dance was one of the first of the dances that asked for fruitfulness in the People. He could see that everyone took this dance very seriously, though some of the women were chortling or giggling at its beginning. He had to concentrate more on the steps, and did not have as much time to look around.

The knaters crowded in closer to the fire for this dancing; their bodies seemed drawn to it, while their shadows leapt up and away, disappearing into the night sky with errant sparks.

The wood selected for the fire was dry and clean burning, so there was not much smoke. But as the dance reached its climax, a cool wind bore down on the fire and forced its way through the glowing logs. Smoke rose and whipped around the beaten back flames. There was a hesitation in the dance beat as everyone looked up and around. Tek quickly glanced ahead and then across the circle. The smoke writhed, blurring the lines between the dancers and their shadows, but Tek thought he saw a man slip in beside Ani for a moment, intimately close, and then leave her side as quickly. And across the circle Okat was dancing with an exaggerated, ferocious intensity that Tek had never seen in a dancing woman before. Her head snapped back and her hands clawed wildly, angrily at the sky. But even before the dancers around Okat could react to her grimacing face and unseemly movements, S'Och cut in beside her and jostled her. Okat abruptly lowered her head and her dancing settled down, becoming more like that of the others again.

After that dance there was a short pause. Then the dancing started up again and with only occasional breaks it went long into the night. The longer and better the dancing, it was believed, the stronger would be the blessings on the knat.

Tek came to identify some of the clanhouse clans by their dancing. A number of the people of S'Kaw's clanhouse seemed to have swooping bird movements. The dancing of other clanhouses reminded Tek of the larger predators of the forest — particularly the moves of the dancers of S'Och's clanhouse. Those mostly resembled the bears to Tek, though sometimes their movements seemed more like those of the feared panther. On the slower dances their steps had a ponderous quality, but when they were aroused by the faster, more intense music and chanting their moves had a surprising swiftness and powerful agility. At these times their moves seemed to flout the norms that all of the other dancers were following. And at these times they exuded a fierce pride that dared anyone else to challenge them about the way they chose to dance.

The dancing of the people of the clanhouse that Ani belonged to was ordinary and restrained. Many of its dancers had a smaller stature and they sought to do only what was required by the dance, with a solemn exactness. They drew no attention to themselves. Tek thought of them as being like the smaller forest animals that survived in part by quietly blending in.

Shortly before dawn the dancing ended and most the knat went to its rest. Tek went to where he and Sho had been guests, but their belongings were no longer there. Tek soon found his own belongings, in a bundle just outside the front doorway of the S'Kaw clanhouse. He picked up the bundle and went inside. Tsihi was busy nearby; she noticed him and told him quickly where to put his things. He was to sleep at the other end of the clanhouse, on the second level with the other boys of about the same age.

Everyone was tired, or feigned tiredness. The clanhouse quickly settled down and almost everyone fell asleep, including Tek. On that first night in his new clan home, he slept a deep and dreamless sleep.

Chapter 3

Tek soon settled into the routines of his new clanhouse and knat.
He worked to be accepted for his own merits — not as his brother's
tag–along. He showed due respect for the knat elders, especially the
chief, the shaman and the clan mothers. He fought the other boys
when he had to, so everyone would know that he could not be
pushed around. He knew his place: like the other boys his age he
generally avoided direct contact with the girls and the women. He
made himself at least as useful as the other boys, mainly by fishing
and by hunting or snaring small game for his clanhouse, which
usually shared the fish and game with the nearby clanhouses. Though
he was often hungry he ate sparingly during the clanhouse meals, not
wanting to get a reputation for being greedy.

In a few short months Tek carved out a decent, fitting place for
himself in the S'Kaw clanhouse of the Ochwah knat. Everyone
seemed to like or at least tolerate him well enough, and he in turn
liked everyone in his own clanhouse, more or less. Some in the
clanhouse were not as pleasant to be around as others. But Tek
found to his relief that neither gross nor petty meanness was typical
among them.

He kept his distance from clan mother S'Kaw; he had done so
ever since his memorable first meeting with her. For her part S'Kaw
seemed to have forgotten that Tek existed. But he knew that at any
time, something could come up that would bring him under her
sharp, direct gaze again. To be prepared for this he studied how
S'Kaw handled everyone and everything. He soon perceived that
S'Kaw was decisive, efficient and ruled the clanhouse with skill and a
minimum of fuss and bother. Largely because of S'Kaw's adeptness
and judgment the clanhouse was a thriving, well ordered place to live.
Tek relaxed somewhat about S'Kaw, and was pleased that his brother
Sho had married a girl of this particular clanhouse.

Tek did not spend much time with his brother after the wedding. Sho was there if he needed him, but he usually went with the men, and when he was in the clanhouse he spent much of his time with his wife, Tsihi.

Tek soon learned that Tsihi was an exceptional young woman. It was not just that she worked hard and worked smart. She also had a lot of what was called the long sight: whatever was happening in the moment was not likely to distract Tsihi from other, perhaps bigger things that were going on. More than once she directed the closing of the main smoke hole, in time enough to keep a sudden downpour from putting out the fire below it. He had also seen her turn away from a distraction in time to keep a child from tumbling into a deep storage pit.

Tsihi was kind to Tek, without seeming to single him out. The day after his first night in the S'Kaw clanhouse, Tsihi quietly gave him a pair of moccasins she had made, which fit him perfectly. He realized that Tsihi had gone to some trouble to get the size of his foot right, without him knowing anything about it. He treasured those moccasins, and repaid Tsihi with his silent but unswerving affection and loyalty.

Tsihi only had to mention during an evening meal that it was about time for the upriver run of bluebacks, and Tek would be out in the river early the next morning with his scap nets, wanting to be among the first to bring some of the silvery, darting fish back to the clanhouse. And he watched and made sure that Tsihi's cache of kindling was never empty. Most in the clanhouse didn't even notice his efforts; those that did sometimes ribbed him with a sly comment, amused by his youthful partiality for his new sister. But because they were among the more astute in the clanhouse, they were quiet and light about it, and Tek felt no reprimand or shame.

Tek had no contact with Okat, the woman he had been warned to avoid, or with hardly anyone else of the S'Och clanhouse. There didn't happen to be any boys around Tek's age in the S'Och clanhouse, which made it easier for Tek to avoid it altogether. But in the same way that Tek studied his clan mother S'Kaw from a distance, he also interested himself in the news of the S'Och clanhouse that filtered through the knat.

Okat featured in much of it. For some time after the weddings, every few days there was news of another of the punishments that Okat meted out to the women who had, at the wedding feast, separated her from Ani and then surrounded her. One by one Okat struck at each of them where they were most vulnerable. For some it was a brutal, lightning–fast physical blow in a tender spot, but Okat's tongue was clearly her most formidable weapon. Her cruel words bit like rattlesnake fangs. After the shock and pain of her cruel words, came the unstoppable swelling of mental discomfort and misery, fomented by her malign insinuations.

One morning, a few days after one such bite, the wounded woman beat her child. What started as a few irritated slaps quickly descended into a terrible, dangerous beating. Okat's poison had festered inside the woman until it erupted that morning over the child's benign clumsiness.

Beating a child was rare, and normally no one interfered with it. But several of the women close by at the time recognized the effects of Okat's poison in the savage blows. They quickly pulled the woman off her child.

Especially after such an incident as that one, Tek wondered why the knat tolerated so much vicious abuse from Okat. Eventually he surmised that it stemmed from a combination of Okat's cold, implacable fury, and her mother's powerful backing. Seemingly blind to Okat's faults, S'Och always came to her aid and defended her, until it became entrenched. Okat's evil became like a sliver too deeply embedded under the skin to ever be removed.

Tek continued to monitor the stories that filtered through the knat about Okat, but as spring progressed into summer all of that seemed to quiet down. Everything seemed normal, except that whenever he happened to see Ani, she was always accompanied by at least three of the other women of her clanhouse. Soon even that seemed to be normal, and since Tek did not expect to have to deal with Okat's evil himself, Okat and her doings gradually receded in his mind.

* * *

18

Tek knew that his life in the S'Kaw clanhouse was about as good as any boy could expect life to be. But as he turned fifteen that summer, an unexpected problem arose.

It was not the rising sap for his manhood. This sprung from the same sap, but it was separate from it and it went a separate, disturbing way inside him.

Tek had the dreams that he knew, from the talk of the older boys, were perfectly normal. He welcomed those dreams: they meant that soon his strength would increase and his man hair would grow in. He looked forward to moving up from fishing and hunting small game in the vicinity of the knat, to the long great hunts of the older boys and men, deep into the forest. And he was determined that whenever there were raids or war, he would be ready for that as well.

But that summer Tek's dreams began to take an odd, terrifying turn.

In the first one Tek was full grown and in a hunting party, stalking deer. The other hunters had spread out beyond his sight and hearing. He was alone as he moved along, alert and silent, with his long man–sized bow ready.

As he concentrated on moving silently, his feet and legs changed. He was elated at first because dream knowledge told him that because of these changes, he was going to be able to move through the forest much more quietly than ever before. But then his arms and hands changed too. His bow and cocked arrow were gone, and he could see that his arms and hands became the thin sturdy legs and the hoofs of a buck.

His front and back legs walked in sync. As he swung his head back to see his hindquarters, he discovered that his head had antlers, when one of the tines brushed a tree branch.

The slight give of the branch against his antler shot an explosive warning through Tek's buck brain and he froze. Hunters were nearby — very skilled hunters. Any movement might expose him to their sight, and to death. Already there was a waft of human scent in the air; Tek carefully shifted an eye in its direction and saw a hunter standing nearly motionless, his arrow just loosed. The dream ended with the arrow at Tek's heart. In the first and most terrifying of those strange hunting dreams, the hunter was his brother Sho.

There were other dreams in which Tek found himself in a huge dark clanhouse. He thought he was alone, but then the knat's hunters came out of the shadows with their knives, advancing with an unmistakable resolve. Dream knowledge told him that though he was standing there as a boy, all of the men could see shadowy antlers floating above his head. Within moments the men surrounded him and were slashing at him.

He woke from these intense, horrifically vivid dreams at their climax with his heart pounding and his body drenched in sweat.

But their aftermath was even worse.

They gave him an irrational fear of everyone. He endured days of feeling disconnected from everything in his past. He hid these feelings as best he could, but the fear drove him to go off into the forest alone every day, creeping back as late as possible each night, until after several days the feelings would fade enough for him to spend more of his daytime around the knat again. On these forest stays he always took his short bow with him, as if going to hunt for small game. But all thoughts of hunting game repelled him now, as much as they had once excited and inspired him.

In the past when the hunters brought a slain deer back from the forest, Tek crowded in with the other boys to hear the fascinating details of the hunt and kill, and to wonder at the hunters' skill in bringing down such a fast and wary animal. But once the strange dreams began, he could no longer revel in the success of a deer hunt. He still made himself go with the other boys to look at the kill, and to stay until the women began their work by stripping the pelt off the flesh. But throughout the ordeal he stared at the dead deer with an internal, kindred horror.

In several of their rituals the People gave thanks to the hunted deer for providing them with so much of the sustenance that they needed. Tek had always accepted this respectful thanksgiving as fair balance against the deer's life. But from the moment in that first dream, when Tek felt his brother's arrow reach his buck heart, he took the deer's part against the People. Try as he may to reason this away, it lodged more deeply into his soul. He could no longer convince himself that the People's thanksgiving was of any value, when measured against the life of the deer.

The inescapable conclusion was to reject his birthright as one of the males of the People, which was to grow up striving to be a valued hunter of his clanhouse and knat. His soul was hopelessly apart, and different from everyone else's. He no longer felt worthy to be one of the People.

He thought about all this and more when he went alone into the forest, on the first days after each of the strange dreams.

He would go far into the forest until he was sure he was alone. Then he usually found a tree with dense foliage to climb into, to hide there and think. But thinking did not help. Only time apart gradually loosened each dream's hold, until after the second or third day he could hope that the strange dreams would stop coming. Then he would be able to forget all this, and his life would right itself again.

Tek sometimes mustered enough resolve to kill a squirrel or a hare, in order to have something to show for his unusually long absences from the knat. During his time in the forest he could have killed many more of them, for as he sat in a tree cloaked in misery, he observed many of the forest's smaller animals as they moved about. But a few token kills were all that he could manage.

He no longer took any pride in his hunting skill, though he did try harder to give the animal a quick death, by a measured accuracy of his shot.

After the miserable days in the forest, he returned to fishing and he fished for as many days as he could, until the next strange dream came and tossed him back into the throes again.

He kept his burden to himself. He acted as normally as possible. The one thing that he could not do though, was eat flesh of a deer. He ate the meat of small game willingly enough, but in his mind, to eat deer flesh would be tantamount to eating his own flesh.

Watching and listening to the others in the clanhouse, he did not think that any of them noticed a difference in him. They treated him the same as always. He continued to hope that his oppressive burden would somehow pass away, though he could not really feel this hope in his heart where it counted. When he looked at everyone else going about their normal lives, he longed for the time before the strange dreams, when he felt connected to them. Now he feared more and more often that he could never fully be a part of their lives again.

Chapter 4

Not long after midsummer the entire knat fairly hummed with the news. Okat's husband Roh had renounced his childless marriage, and moved himself and his belongings over to the clanhouse that Ani lived in. Roh and Ani would not be formally wedded until the knat's next wedding ceremony, but they were a couple now. Little Ani's belly was beginning to expand with their child.

Okat had always treated her husband Roh very well during their marriage: for him she sheathed her claws, and sweetened her tongue. But eventually it became clear that together Okat and Roh could not have what Roh had come to want most of all, which was a child of his own.

Roh was a lazy man, who had gone much to seed since marrying Okat. Pampered by his wife and her mother, he had allowed his hunting and warrior skills — which had never been great to begin with — to atrophy. He enjoyed the ease of his life — his comfortable, privileged place in the knat that he had not had to work for.

For a while Roh had accepted the absence of a child from his and Okat's union as a sorrow meted out to him by life. But as he watched the children of the other men growing straight and true under the contented gaze of their fathers, he began to chaff against this fate. He decided to find out for certain whether it was the seed of his loins, or the womb in his wife's belly, that was the obstacle. He decided to find out by trysting with another woman.

Roh told himself that if the fault was with his seed, he would be content and would thereafter magnanimously live out his years with Okat. He did not give much thought to what would happen if instead he was virile, and the failure of their union was with Okat.

Roh did not know what some in the knat had long known: a year or so after Roh and Okat married, Okat secretly bullied the most virile man in the knat into trysting with her long and fully enough, until she was quite certain that it was she who lacked what was needed to make a child.

Roh would have preferred to tryst with a woman who had already been married and given birth. He knew of several likely women, including some who had not yet remarried after their husbands had died or had left them. But in the end it was Ani. She was the only woman who was foolish enough to secretly tryst with him. The others he approached either were not interested in him, or were much too afraid of what Okat would do when she eventually found out about it. Roh tried to cajole them, telling them that Okat would not necessarily ever find out, but none of them could be swayed.

One day near the end of the previous winter Ani had come upon Roh sighing by the river, pretending to fish. He was especially unhappy that day, and he looked it. Ani made the mistake of stopping and asking him what was the matter.

At the sound of Ani's voice, Roh took in her small form and trusting eyes in one quick glance, and he unerringly selected the right hook to play her in. He worked on her sympathy, slumping his shoulders more dejectedly, keeping his voice low and sad as he poured his sorrows into her ears. Then he subtly flattered the plain, overlooked girl, telling her of the beauty he could see in her that others had missed.

Ani rose quickly, eagerly to his bait. Before long they were trysting.

They should never have begun it. But neither Roh nor Ani had any of the long sight.

On the day before the knat's next wedding ceremony — on the same day that Sho and Tek arrived at the knat with their belongings, Ani told Roh that she thought she was carrying his child.

Though Roh had long hoped to have a child, this news caught him completely by surprise. Somehow he had always thought that it was probably his seed that had been at fault. He had also been thinking about ending his trysts with Ani, by going away on one of the longer hunts and then not resuming the trysts when he got back. He had always been a little repelled by how easy Ani had been to catch, and during their lovemaking he was beginning to find some of her little pawing gestures irritating.

Ani's news changed everything. Of course she could not be certain yet, but as Roh looked down into her flushed, pleased face he saw a real beauty in her for the first time. It was unmistakably the beauty of a woman whose body carries a child.

Roh had a rare flash of insight. Against all expectation, he saw that this little Ani was probably going to give him what he had come to want so much. And for the first time in his life, Roh felt the deep mating love for a woman.

Neither Roh or Ani could hide their frothy, distracted happiness from those who knew them best. Okat was one of the first to find out about it. Roh braced himself for her wrath. Though he had never yet been the target of its power, he had seen her wielding it against others often enough. He was guarded and apprehensive, but in the days and weeks that followed Okat did not attack him. Instead, she acted very sorrowful and wronged whenever she was with him. Roh did not believe that her pathos was real. But he realized that as long as Okat thought he would not leave her, he would be safe from her ruthless ire.

Ani did not fare so well. There was the ugly scene at the wedding feast: Okat's vicious tongue left so many deep cuts in little Ani's heart that night, that despite Ani's determination to rejoice in the morsel of life growing inside her, her newfound happiness nearly left her. For many painful weeks afterward, Okat's cruel words echoed endlessly in Ani's small simple mind. And in Ani's dreams Okat's fierce face lunged at her again and again.

Ani also suffered acutely as each of the women who had come to her aid that night, fell prey to Okat's cruelty. Each time that Okat got to another one of them and drubbed the woman in a way that wounded deepest and hurt the most, Ani cringed and cried as if she herself had been struck.

But each and every one of the women was a survivor. Most of them were in Ani's close family and lived in the same clanhouse with her. A few even tried to comfort Ani when they saw that Okat's vengeance on them was upsetting her so much, even though they all wished fruitlessly that Ani had not brought this trouble and danger upon her clanhouse. It would all pass, these comforters told Ani.

24

She must not think of it now. She must not let it mark the child inside her. She must keep her head down, and keep herself healthy and safe, for the child's sake. Ani took some comfort from them, and did her best to follow their advice.

But when one of the women, maimed by Okat's vicious words, nearly beat her precious child to death, Ani's head came up. How, she wondered aloud to the other women in the clanhouse, had one evil woman, who wasn't even the clan mother in her own clanhouse, come to rule in this way over the entire knat? For Okat did rule, Ani argued in her small tremulous voice. Okat ruled by cruelty, and with S'Och by her side no one, not even the chief, dared to cross her. Could they not all see this? Surely if they all joined together there was something they could do to stop Okat?

The women listened to Ani with one ear only. Ani had always had a low place among them. She was a pleasant enough young woman, but her work was sloppy and skimpy, and from her talk they had decided long ago that her mind was not at all deep or interesting. When the clanhouse found to its surprise that Ani was with child, and with none other than the husband of the formidable Okat, everyone grimly resolved that it was going to be their duty to try to protect Ani and the child from Okat, to the best of their ability. But it would not go any further than that.

What Ani was saying now in the privacy of the clanhouse, about directly challenging Okat — it was an unthinkable undertaking. They all knew in their bones that even if all them joined together to fight Okat, she and her protective mother S'Och would still be much too powerful for them. It was a crazy idea — as crazy as if all the hares in a meadow banded together to fight two bears. There was no doubt about who would win. No, Ani's talk was just the goofy prattle that sometimes came out of the mouth of a newly expectant mother. The women paid no attention to it.

After Okat accosted Ani at the wedding, the clanhouse made the decision to guard Ani from Okat. To make this feasible, Ani's clan mother ordered Ani to always stay in the immediate vicinity of the clanhouse, except when she would be allowed to go and work in the planting fields, together with all the other able–bodied women. Nothing more. Ani begged to be allowed to go gathering by the river and to go berry and herb gathering, but this was firmly forbidden.

The clan mother also required that when Ani went to the planting fields, three or four of the women of the clanhouse were to always accompany her, close in, to guard her. The clan mother obtained the chief's approval for this, and then it was announced publicly so that all of the other clanhouses were made aware of it. It was understood that as long as these guards did nothing to provoke anyone, any harm that came to them would be treated as a serious affront to their entire clanhouse.

Clan mother S'Och objected vociferously to this odd arrangement. "There is nothing going on in this knat that cannot be taken care of in the usual ways," she growled. "They are finding deep murky shadows where there is nothing at all but the clearest light of day," she huffed. "It is ridiculous and insulting to all the other clanhouses, and should not be tolerated." S'Och called on the other clan mothers to back her up in her objections, but one after another they warily declined. They said among themselves that, "When the panther hunts, the People must sleep with their long bows ready. Even the bear must sleep with its claws outward."

About a dozen of the women rotated the guard duty. It was an added burden that, though shared, was not likely to end anytime soon, and it kept them all from getting their other work done as quickly and as well as they liked. It was an arduous, irritating chore. And despite the special arrangement made by their clan mother, they all worried that this guard work could prove to be dangerous to them, if Okat took it too personally against them. Though they were backed by their entire clanhouse, and were only doing what was required of them, there was no knowing what someone like Okat might do. Though the women did not shirk their guard work, they were unhappy about it and grumbled among themselves.

Ani's world contracted sharply. As the days of being guarded wore on and on, Ani especially came to hate it because she was never allowed to meet with Roh. As soon as the women guarding her saw him, they forced Ani away in another direction. But though Ani hated it she understood and accepted her clanhouse's precautions. She had only to glimpse Okat glaring at her from the other side of the planting field, to feel the mindless terror of a cornered animal. For it was easy for her to see that Okat's fury against her had not abated, and she feared that it only grew stronger.

By midsummer the fields around the knat and the forest reached their most fulsome greening. And the small bump swelling in Ani's belly became unmistakable. Roh got a good look at it one day from where he lay hiding to watch his wife and Ani and practically all of the other knat women on their way to the fields, for the weeding and grubbing. When he saw that bump, he decided that he could no longer live apart from Ani, his one true love.

He strode back to the knat, gathered his belongings, and took them to the clanhouse of Ani's family. He then visited the chief and the shaman, and told them of his decision. The chief advised him gravely, to be very certain of himself before he acted. But the shaman went further. The shaman spoke firmly against Roh's decision to leave Okat. This gave Roh a few moments of doubt, but he swept them aside. He could not be turned back from what he had decided.

He was standing beside the front end of the S'Och clanhouse when Okat and her mother S'Och returned from the fields that day. The chief and two of his sons stood a short distance away — close enough to witness Roh's public renouncement of his marriage with Okat, but signaling by the distance they took no active part in the proceeding.

Neither S'Och or Okat made any effort to change Roh's mind. S'Och gazed balefully at the man who had just completely destroyed the happiness of her precious daughter. Okat had apparently decided to maintain a sorrowful face. But this facade, so scrupulously maintained day in and day out for so long, fell apart just as Roh finished speaking. He saw a wildness flicker in his former wife's eyes, and a threatening flash of her teeth as her mouth twisted in a grotesque grimace. His words of farewell guttered out as he backed away from the two women.

When he joined Ani they had a joyful reunion. Ani prattled nonstop while Roh draped himself over her openly, for everyone to see how genuine his love for her was.

Arrangements were made in the clanhouse for Roh and Ani to have a living compartment near its center. It was a better position in the clanhouse than Ani deserved, but the clan mother ordered it even though it displaced several much more worthy family units. The clan mother took no chances. She would keep this silly, heedless couple close to the heart of the clanhouse, as a precaution for their safety.

Roh swiftly ingratiated himself in his new clanhouse. Invigorated by being with the love of his life and with the coming of their child, he hunted better and was more helpful and companionable than he had been for many years. The clanhouse accepted him, as they accepted everything — the good and the bad, the joyous and the devastating. They did not begrudge Roh his happiness, yet they nervously watched for the storm that he was surely bringing with him.

When Roh was not fulfilling men's duties, he took over the work of guarding Ani as often as he could. And sometimes, contrary to the clan mother's strict orders, he took Ani berry picking, or he let her gather along the river while he fished close by. At these times he always went armed with his long bow, calling it just a precaution in case they should happen upon a frothing wolf or bear. Close to the knat he practiced openly and often with his long bow. Soon everyone knew that Roh was a rather good shot again.

For a while after Roh's move, nothing out of the ordinary happened to anyone in the clanhouse. Roh and Ani began to feel safer as the high and bright summer days passed. They suggested to the clan mother that she could relax the guard on Ani, but she refused to do this. "You are taking foolish risks," she warned them severely. "You should not allow yourselves to be lulled by Okat's unusual restraint." Chastened by her vehemence, they took more precautions, though not as many as the clan mother advised. They were still happy in each other, and though they lived under the ever–present threat that Okat might strike at any time, that threat had lost some of its power over them.

By the end of the summer days Okat's temper had been so cool and quiet for so long that the knat began to have an unfamiliar sense of normalcy. Several times Okat even turned her back on provocations that in the recent past would have been certain to cause an eruption of viciousness. Apart from an occasional glare or a sudden irritated slap, Okat largely maintained the sorrowful mien of a grievously wronged woman, absorbed in nursing her wounded heart.

While everyone tried to enjoy the unexpected change in Okat, the wiser heads of the knat did not believe that the calm was genuine, or that it would last. It had an ominous feel to it. They did not believe that Okat, who had never let any slight go unpunished, could change in this fundamental aspect of her nature. They knew she was incapable of feeling anything for others. She always had been that way, and she always would be so. No, this odd calm only meant that Okat was being unusually patient and circumspect. And they feared that the longer it took the new Okat to mete out her punishments, the worse they were going to be.

Chapter 5

In the early fall Tek walked as a shapeshifter for the first time.

By the end of the summer his strange, intense dreams came so frequently, that if he spent several days in the forest after each of them, he would never be able to leave it.

So he unwisely resolved to stop going to the forest altogether. Somehow, he decided, he must learn to manage without the forest's healing balm.

But staying out of the forest only made things very much worse. The dreams came nearly every night and he was in a bleary stupor when awake. He tried to catch fish and help out with chores, but a pounding in his head was like a drumbeat for a chant that ran nonstop in his mind — that he was no longer one of the People. He had a buck's inborn fear of the People. He could never hunt deer like he was supposed to. It would be like hunting his own self.

At times he tottered with sudden dizziness, and a feeling seized him, that his flesh was about to fall off his bones.

Every day he felt more tightly bound by the strange dreams. He began to think confusedly of doing the unthinkable: of going far from the knat and living in the forest apart from the People, for the rest of his life. But he held on a little longer, groggy by day and nearly sleepless at night, still hoping against hope that the dreams would somehow, like a spent storm, pass away . . . dissipating into nothingness.

Then came the night when Tek had a new, completely different dream.

First came some restful sleep — the first in several nights, and then he dreamt that while he was sleeping aloft with the other boys, an insistent call from the forest woke him, that only he could hear. He got up and began to climb down the notched log to the clanhouse's dirt floor. But partway down he lost his hand holds and footing; a panicky feeling shot through him as he realized that he had no grip because he was turning into a buck. He twisted and fell the rest of the way. His four hooves hit the dirt floor with a quiet thud.

Frozen with instinctive fear, he was inundated with the fulsome scents of everyone and everything in the clanhouse. The odors floated and mingled together, all incredibly strong and distinct, unlike anything he had been able to smell before. And the strongest scents of all — easily overpowering the scent of earth, wood and hide — were those of the beings asleep all around him in the living compartments — dangerous beings that, when they were awake, avidly hunted deer, and casually cut up deer carcasses.

Tek flicked his buck ears and with his greatly enhanced hearing he listened for sounds meaning one of these beings was awake and knew he was there. There was nothing, except the faint rustlings of bodies turning in sleep, and the cadences of quiet snores, to disturb the dream's silence.

He had excellent night vision as a buck; he saw no threatening movement in the moonlight coming through the open smoke holes. He was safe for the moment.

He tried desperately to turn himself from a buck back into a boy, but he could not make it happen. He knew he was still partly of the People, because in his own scent he smelled the boy Tek as well as the buck that he had become. But an overwhelming fear of the People trapped him in his buck form.

His only thought was to get out of this clanhouse, and the knat. To survive he must reach the safety of the forest.

The entranceway in the knat's high log wall was lashed tightly shut, making it impossible for him to leave the knat that way. But some racks lined the inside of the knat's wall, in a place that got a lot of the autumn's afternoon sun, for the drying of meats and chunks of squash. The racks were sturdy; Tek thought that if he could get out of this clanhouse and take a great running leap up onto one of them, he might be able to spring high enough to clear the knat's wall.

An instinct to stay motionless, in the midst of the danger that surrounded him, kept Tek frozen in place. His boy mind reasoned frantically with his buck mind, to convince it that the only chance to survive was to move rather than stay still. Finally he was able to take one cautious step, and then another. He headed down the aisle toward the clanhouse's main door at the other end of the clanhouse.

The smaller back door was closer, but its hide covering was lashed more tightly shut for the night, and as a buck he would not be able to open it. The vent flaps beside it were full open but they were much too high and small for him to get through them. The main door was his only way out. Its lashings were always looser; he hoped they would be loose enough for him to ease himself through a gap between the hide flap and the door frame.

With every step that Tek took in this dream he felt himself walking further and further away from the life he had known as one of the People. Whether he got out of the knat alive or was felled by a hunter's arrow, life as he knew it was over. The strong odors of the sleepers, especially the men, pulsed off them and swirled thickly around him. He marveled that his own strong scent did not alert a light sleeper to his foreign presence, until he remembered that the People could not smell things nearly as well as most of the forest animals could.

As he passed through the center of the clanhouse he got an unusually strong and distinct whiff of *bird* from two of the family compartments. Most of the compartment flaps were down, but some were up for better airing. He knew the smell of feathers from before this dream. But now as a buck he could smell that these were not cast off feathers; they throbbed with what would have to be the smell of a living bird.

As Tek puzzled about this oddity there was a faint rustling noise from his brother and Tsihi's compartment. He froze for long seconds, until the rustling quieted into stillness.

He made it the rest of the way down the central aisle, but a problem arose when he reached the main door. He had thought he could squeeze his narrow buck body through one of the gaps between the hide door flap and its frame, but he had completely forgotten about — his antlers! He couldn't see them, so to determine their size he extended his neck cautiously and rubbed the antler tines very lightly against the door flap. His antlers were much too wide, jutting from the front and sides of his head — the tines were bound to get caught in the strips of lashing.

Tek knew that with some powerful strokes of his sharp hooves he could puncture the thick bark wall beside the door. But the tearing, ripping noise would surely wake up the clanhouse, and perhaps some who slept in the nearby clanhouses. Not certain whether to risk this or not, Tek pawed at the hide door's lashing where the gap was largest, to see if he could widen the gap enough to get his antlers through.

He was concentrating on a loose tangle of knots when a silent wing brushed past his nose, and a small owl landed on the bottom of the vent opening above and to one side of the door. The owl stared down at him with its great round eyes. Its head jerked a little, sideways and back, as its small beak fluttered open and shut. Then it fluffed all of its feathers and shook them back down again.

It was about then that Tek began to understand that this new, long dream was not a dream at all. He had really turned into a buck, and he really could not get out of this clanhouse because his antlers were much too wide and pointy. He also knew that the little owl staring back at him was Tsihi, wife of his brother.

He shared the People's fearful awe of owls, as messengers of death. But his qualms stilled; this owl was not just any owl. It was beloved Tsihi.

But he stood there with the mix of owl and Tsihi scent in his nostrils, completely at a loss. Tsihi seemed to understand his predicament. She eyed the gap; she eyed his antlers. She bobbed her head at him, and she turned herself around in a complete circle where she perched.

Tek did nothing but continue to stare at her. She repeated the maneuver deliberately twice more. Each time the bob of her head got a little sharper. Finally Tek thought he understood. He quietly turned himself around, so that his hindquarters were facing the door instead of his head, and looked over his shoulder at her.

Tsihi flew down and lightly nipped one of his hocks. He raised that leg and tried to get its hoof up to where it could go backward through the gap between the frame post and door flap. To help him find the gap with his back leg Tsihi fluttered and nipped. Tek felt the nips, but her fluttering wings made no sound.

Once Tek got one back leg part of the way through the gap, he wanted to get it all the way through, but Tsihi signaled him to stop

33

that by a sharper nip and then lightly nipped his other back leg. Tek understood: one leg all the way through would tighten the gap too much for him to get the other leg through. He was going to have to get both back legs partly through first. He managed this with Tsihi's help, even though the narrow space between the doorframe and the edge of the door flap tightened alarmingly below his rump. The rubbing against the fur of his back legs made him panicky. With great difficulty he forced down the urge to kick wildly and lash out with his hooves.

Wriggling, twisting, pushing and arching under Tsihi's guidance Tek slowly squeezed his hindquarters through the gap. His nerves were about to snap, from the unnaturalness of backing up, the confining pressure on his sides, and the wretched scraping of frame, hide and lacings against the nap of his fur. And unable to see what was outside, he felt completely exposed and vulnerable.

If only he could turn himself back into a boy. He prayed and wished and tried for it fervently, but he remained a buck, as Tsihi fluttered and nipped with more determination than before. He also wished that Tsihi could simply turn back into a woman, and untie the door flap for him. But deep inside himself he understood that if she was anywhere near him in her woman form his control would dissolve and he really would go berserk. Tsihi must have known this as well. Never once did her woman scent become stronger than her owl scent.

They had just gotten to the tricky part of easing his antlered head through, when there was a faint rustling noise coming from the center of the clanhouse. With their sharp hearing they both heard it: Tek froze and Tsihi abruptly landed on his antlers. The noise got a little louder. Tek still could not identify it but Tsihi flew off toward it. After she reached it, the noise stopped and Tek thought he could hear some whispering.

Tsihi returned; the noise did not resume. The work of easing the antlers through the gap began, and proceeded with excruciating slowness. Going backward through the gap kept the tips of Tek's antlers from catching in the lacing, but even so Tek had to twist his head sideways, and contort his neck, and tug in ways that he had not thought possible. But by then he trusted Tsihi's directions implicitly.

At last with a sharp tug his antlers pulled free and he was fully outside the clanhouse.

Tek had been taking in the scents outside the clanhouse ever since his nose was through the gap. He smelled nothing that he thought would be unusual. Nor did he hear anything unusual, and there was no immediate danger in what he was able to see during his head's strenuous maneuvers to free his antlers.

But as soon as he got his head up and turned himself fully around, he was shocked to his marrow to see the clan mother S'Och standing a short distance away. Dressed in her ceremonial clan mother robes. Silently watching him.

Tsihi landed on his antlers, and uttered a low odd kwiiit. Tek could not understand its meaning exactly, but from the compounding impossibilities that had been turning out to be realities, Tek's understanding expanded enough for him to make some sense of this too. The being that was standing there looked like S'Och, but it was not S'Och. An essential part of her was missing, because this being had no scent, and when it moved slightly there was no sound at all from the knocking together of the bear claws sewn across the breast of her robe.

If S'Och had been fully there, Tek was certain that she would not have simply stood there looking back at him. She would have called out to rouse hunters to come and kill him. Even as she was now, Tek could see in her eyes a lust to kill any and all deer within the swipe of her great bear claws.

That was another difference between this apparition and the real S'Och: the bearlike qualities that Tek had noticed before in S'Och were unmistakable now in the heavy set of the brow and prominent nose, and the burly curve of her shoulders and arms. Her fingers, curving slightly, flexed like lethal bear claws below the long sleeves of her robe.

But without any scent of the People or of bear, Tek had no fear of her, at least not yet. He did not know how to classify her, so he made something up. He thought of her as some kind of dreamwalker.

A huge hawk flapped down, pulling up sharply and landing in front of the S'Kaw clanhouse. S'Och stared at the hawk as if she was quite surprised to see it there. But while Tsihi pecked at Tek to move him away in the direction of the drying racks, S'Och approached the hawk and knelt to sit formally in front of it. In the moments before Tek turned away, he saw the hawk and S'Och bow slightly toward each other, as if to begin some silent communion with each other.

A very faint lightening in the sky showed just above the knat's walls. Dawn was coming. Muted noises came from several of the clanhouses. People were beginning to stir.

Tek sniffed and nudged the drying racks. Sturdy as they were, he was not sure whether they would be steady enough for the solid spring he needed, to get up and over the wall. The racks might sway or collapse under his weight. And if his hooves slipped between the slats spaced along the top of the racks, his legs would get caught. This attempt to spring over the wall from these racks could end in disaster, but he was going to have to try it anyway. Any moment now an early riser would come out of a nearby clanhouse and see him.

Tsihi flew a pattern over the racks, showing Tek what she thought was his best route up and over. But as Tek gauged the path she laid out, he could not agree with her. He had not questioned her judgment when she helped him escape from the clanhouse, but in this matter he would have to choose his own way. Tsihi as a light, fluttering bird could not possibly make the necessary allowances for his weight, and for the dynamics of his spring.

He selected the racks that he intended to leap onto and then spring upward from. He gave them some final testing nudges, not letting himself think about what would happen if they shifted, or if his legs got jammed down between the slats.

He wheeled away and moved as quickly and silently as he could until he reached the place he had chosen to start his run toward the racks. It was near the center of the knat, nearly halfway across it from the racks. Several clanhouses blocked his view of the racks, but he needed that much running distance to get a feel for the power in his legs, and to build up enough speed for his leap.

Pausing for just a moment before starting his run, Tek remembered the insistent call of the forest that had woken him, right before he became a buck. He tried to set his recollection of it firmly in his mind, hoping it would help him clear the wall. Nose high, he caught the first traces of the forest's new day in the breeze floating over the knat's high wall. And with it came the call, stronger than

36

ever before. His spirit surged to get to the forest that was calling him home.

His run began. For the first time he felt the full stretch and power of his legs. The earth gave and then pushed back beneath his hooves. Despite the danger, despite his wild fear of this place and his urgent need to escape it, Tek felt a wonder at his strength and agility as a buck.

The thud of his hooves striking earth broke the predawn silence. It was a dull, heavy sound that did not belong in a knat of the People. It seemed shatteringly loud and discordant to Tek, and it gave him a frisson as if the entire knat woke up immediately and in another moment would be closing in on him.

His legs stretched their farthest. His hooves bit earth. He bore down on the racks and made his great desperate leap.

His front legs hit the rack he had chosen; it shivered under him. With momentum from the run he just barely got his hind legs up onto the rack behind his front legs. His front legs slithered between the slats; his back hooves scrambled madly for a footing. The rack leaned away from the wall. He bunched his muscles for his leap upward toward the wall, but he knew his back legs did not have enough spring in them to clear it. He knew at that moment that he was not going to make it to the forest.

But he had reckoned without the hawk. As he made his desperate leap off the rack the hawk was suddenly a great black arrow diving out of the sky, raking his left flank with its talons and gouging his hind legs above the hocks with its hooked beak. The surprise, shock and pain of it propelled Tek skyward; he cleared the wall, though the roughly pointed tops of the logs scraped his belly and shanks cruelly as he passed over them.

The instant he landed outside the knat wall he raced westward through the cleared land to reach the forest. At the forest edge he felt safe enough to pause and look back. The knat's tall spiky wall was silhouetted against early light. The hawk was perched on the top of it, on one of the pointed log tips, watching him sullenly. It gave a long shrill cry that rang in Tek's head long after he had run far away, up into the forested mountains, far enough away from the river and the knats stippled along it to feel safe from the People's hunters.

Chapter 6

Tek spent six days in the forest. By the end of the third day, in the blessed calm and stillness of the higher forest, he found out how to change himself back and forth between boy and buck. It was rapid and not difficult at all, once he understood himself better, and was at peace with himself.

He also found that all the other deer avoided him: his own scent had too much of the People in it for them to accept him. He veered away from the few paths that bore the scent of bear or panther. He did not come across any roaming wolf packs; at this plentiful time of year most of them hunted further down the mountain.

He ranged and foraged alone, learning the forest in new ways, and reveling in his buck life. But there was a sadness too. He was always going to be of both worlds — that of the People and that of the forest — and would never fully belong to either of them.

He thought about Tsihi being both a woman of the knat and an owl, and about how she spent most of her life as one of the People, rather than as an owl.

Her owlness seemed quite natural to Tek, even fitting. But Tek's buck shape was all at odds: it was unnatural to be both one of the People, and its primary prey.

He thought about the hawk. Everything had happened too fast for him to fully get its person scent. He was only sure that the hawk was someone of the S'Kaw clanhouse.

Near the end of the third day he felt able to go back to the knat. And he was keen to talk with Tsihi about this shapeshifting. He also wanted to find out who the hawk was.

It would take him another three days to reach the knat. He travelled as a buck during the day, east out of the mountains. At night he became a boy and slept in a tree. He gained confidence that he would spot a hunting party long before it knew he was there.

Unlike the strange hunting dreams that had always ended with the hunters killing him, he felt he had the advantage now, for he was no ordinary deer. Besides having a deer's keen senses and reflexes, he also had his knowledge of the People, to use against their hunter ways. At worst, if they came too close and he could not melt away, he could turn himself back into a boy, before they actually saw him.

It was early in the morning of his fourth day in the forest, that he saw the dreamwalker S'Och again. As before she was without scent, and was soundless.

She was walking by herself through the forest, dressed in her ceremonial robes. Her face looked frightened and anxious — so unlike her in real life. She was heading generally westward, but while Tek watched she veered both northerly and southerly, and at times turned completely around. She halted often and looked around, dazed, as if she could not be certain of which way to go.

When S'Och noticed Tek there as a buck, she frowned warningly at him to come no closer. But her fingers did not flex and there was no prey–killing urge in her eyes. Tek simply kept his distance as she meandered past him.

He turned himself back into a boy when he got close to the knat, late in the afternoon of the sixth day. Before long he met some of the younger boys, who were returning to the knat with some squirrel kill. They were a rough bunch that he did not usually have much to do with. None of them were from the S'Kaw clanhouse; they might not even know that he'd been gone for six days.

He was naked but joined the boys boldly, responding to their stares by telling them that he'd lost his breechcloth and fishing gear in a bad tumble by the river. Some large rocks he'd been climbing over far upriver had suddenly shifted and rolled out from under him. He spoke brusquely, convincingly. He had always been a truthful boy; he was a little surprised by how quickly and smoothly the web of lies spun from his lips.

His lies sounded plausible to the younger boys: he certainly looked like he had been through what he described. He had many days–old bruises on his legs and lower arms. His left side, his stomach and the front of his thighs were deeply gouged. Puncture wounds above the backs of his knees were crusted with blood, and festering.

When Tek had turned back into a boy each night in the forest, he found that he still had much of the enhanced sense of smell, sight and hearing of a buck. As he returned to the knat with the boys he kept a distance from them, unsettled by their stronger scent that as a buck he associated with hunters, and with death.

Before they reached the knat, from the boys' talk Tek learned that the knat was in mourning. S'Och had died in the same night that Tek had first become a buck. From this Tek realized that that there was no such thing as what he had dubbed a dreamwalker. While he was a buck, it was S'Och's departing spirit that he had seen, first on the night that she died, and later on its journey west to the spirit lands.

As they neared the knat he saw the women in the fields some distance away, working on the maize harvest. Tsihi and other women of the S'Kaw clanhouse would be there. He was nearly bursting with impatience to talk with Tsihi, but it would not be fitting for him to try to approach her there.

The high knat walls loomed closer; he braced himself for the barrage of hunter scent that would inundate and buffet him inside the knat.

Upon rounding the knat wall and reaching the entranceway, Tek saw a small boy of the S'Kaw clanhouse get up and come to them. The boy had been given the simple but boring task of watching for Tek's return. Now his little chest swelled with importance. As soon as he told Tek that he was to go immediately to their clanhouse, the boy turned and ran inside the knat to report that Tek was back.

The S'Och clanhouse, which was close to the knat's entrance, bore all the insignia of mourning. Condolence sticks from the other clanhouses lay on a low framework that had been constructed a short distance from the front of the main door. The higher up air flaps of the clanhouse were open, but the door hides at each end were down. The odor of juniper burning inside the clanhouse hung heavy in the air around it. As Tek passed the clanhouse a low wail from inside broke the heavy silence surrounding it.

Long before Tek reached the S'Kaw clanhouse, two of its men came up beside him. They came quietly from between other clanhouses along his route and flanked him, as if they thought he might try to bolt away from them. One of the men was S'Kaw's husband Tehwe; the other was one of his younger grandsons. Tek took in their scents; though he could detect no bird scent in either of them, he looked with some wariness at the hawk–like curve of Tehwe's nose.

Inside the clanhouse Tehwe motioned Tek to follow him into a compartment reserved for tending to the very sick. It was isolated from the other compartments; it was used for storage when it was not occupied, as were the compartments closest to it. Tehwe told his grandson to let the shaman in when he arrived, but to keep everyone else from disturbing them. He lowered the compartment's flaps, sat down facing Tek, and spoke in a voice just barely above a whisper.

"There are a very few among the People who are shapeshifters. You, I hear, are one of them. You, I hear, became a buck for the first time six days ago."

Tehwe paused, waiting for Tek to acknowledge what he had just said. Tek nodded, and Tehwe slowly nodded back in confirmation of Tek's admission.

"Can you take any other shape?"

"No," Tek replied. "Only a buck."

It seemed to Tek that Tehwe was relieved to hear that he had only one shape. But Tehwe told him that he might, at some time in the future, find that he could take another shape.

"For now, though," Tehwe told him, "this by itself is going to be bad enough."

The knat's shaman arrived, and Tehwe parted the flaps for him to climb into the compartment.

"A buck, eh?" the shaman said sourly as soon as he was seated. He eyed Tek with disfavor.

Tek soon understood that the shaman was very angry with him, for not going to him about his strange dreams. In harsh whispers the shaman peppered Tek with questions about the dreams. Tek answered them, and tried to convey how the dreams had made him feel apart from the People, though he used the word for 'unworthy' rather than 'apart', hoping this deviation from the truth would soothe the irritated shaman. He also managed to slip in that because the shaman still hunted, he had greatly feared that if he had gone to the shaman, the shaman would have immediately put an arrow through his heart, instead of helping him. He spun another lie into this by

41

exaggerating the shaman's prowess as a hunter. As soon as that lie was out of his mouth he worried that it had been too flattering, too obvious. He could see by a cautionary flash in Tehwe's eyes that Tehwe thought so too. But the shaman calmed down noticeably, basking in the lie's false beauty. Tek breathed a little more slowly and evenly.

Even so there was a ragged catch in his breath, and he felt increasingly hot and dull. A fever had been rising in him for days, from the festering wounds on the back of his thighs.

The shaman and Tehwe both saw how feverish he was. The shaman told him that he was to come to him for instruction when — if — he got better. And he told Tehwe to summon him immediately if anything untoward happened in the meantime. Tek did not know what the shaman meant by that, but Tehwe nodded curtly, and the shaman left.

Within moments the compartment's flaps parted from the outside. Clan mother S'Kaw, the only person in the clanhouse who could flout Tehwe's orders with impunity, elbowed the flaps farther apart and stood there with a bowl in each hand. The scent of a bird of prey — of a hawk — rolled off her, mixing with her woman scent.

She was bristling with fury. She was much angrier with him than the shaman had been. Tek thought confusedly that no lie could deflect *this* much anger. In his mind, struggling against the soaring fever, he heard echoes of the harsh screech of the hawk six days earlier, from atop the knat wall, as it watched him bound into the forest.

"Stupid boy!" S'Kaw hissed at him. "Thought you could heal yourself?! On your own?! You should have come back days ago!"

Tehwe took the bowls from S'Kaw. She climbed in and took charge. She allowed Tek to have a few sips of water from one of the bowls, then she ordered him to lie on his stomach, prodding him over and down in his heavy slowness. The swelling puncture wounds on the backs of his thighs were cleansed with the rest of the water, and the salve in the other bowl was worked deeply, painfully into the wounds.

The fever seized Tek and swept him away on a broad unknown river. Sometimes the river's water felt so cold that Tek's body convulsed as he shivered violently and helplessly. Other times he was so hot that he baked like a log snagged high and parch dry in the sun.

Time and time again he rose to a wretched consciousness, when the backs of his thighs were pummeled by strong hands. The merciless hands forced foul puss out of the puncture wounds, and salve into them.

Sometimes the river of fever nudged him into shallows, where he floated peacefully for a while. Then someone flipped him over and disrupted his peace until he sipped some water.

Inexorably the river drew him into its strongest, most dangerous current. He bobbed in and out of it, barely held back from its swift downward flow, as if tethered by nothing more than a raveling strand of spider silk.

Deliriums and terrible dreams battered him as he bobbed in and out of that dark current.

In the worst of these terrors he was always a buck, with a shadowy creature tearing at his entrails. He could not tell if the creature was delirium, or terrible dreams. He wanted desperately to know which it was, for deliriums lie, while dreams had kernels of truth.

Truth was crucially important to him. Recently, fundamental impossibilities had become realities. He now yearned to distinguish eddies of truth, from torrents of lies, and the yearning burned hotter in him than the fever.

Frail and battered, he prayed from his heart for truths, no matter how terrible they might be. But his prayer, steeped in delirium, was not granted.

The capricious river of fever swelled on, feeling broad and endless until, in an instant, it burst into thousands of rivulets, and sank into earth. Tek was left lying limp and weak in a hazy dream of warm moist land, with a cool freshening breeze wafting over his back.

He had been lost to the fever for two days. If the shaman had ever been summoned to him during that time, he was not aware of it.

Chapter 7

The entire knat was subdued during the ten days of the mourning for S'Och. A mourning was an especially sacred time when it was a chief or one of the clan mothers who had died. All of the clan mothers were important, though some were more so than others.

S'Och had been a very important clan mother — strong and influential. She was not nearly as old as some of the others, but she had left her mark not only on her own clanhouse but on most of the others, in many ways.

One was the way that she used her strength and position to force the knat to accept the violence and viciousness of her favorite daughter Okat. In public S'Och always excused Okat, even when she acknowledged in private that Okat had done wrong. Each time that Okat struck, S'Och bent and twisted the blame until it fell, however ill fittingly, more on the victim's shoulders than on her daughter's. She was always the roused mother bear towering over her small, defenseless cub. Time and time again the knat lowered its eyes and backed away from that danger.

S'Och's death had not been expected. She had seemed well and vigorous. No one had seen or dreamed any omens that would, in retrospect, have foretold it.

The women of S'Och's clanhouse laid out her best clothing for her Beyond journey. Women of the other clanhouses came and prepared the body, dressing it and then wrapping it tightly in a whitened deer skin shroud. A small opening was left in the shroud near S'Och's head, so that if her spirit was still resident, it could get out when it was ready to leave. Her shrouded body was placed beside the center hearth of her clanhouse, with the feet toward the west door.

The first evening after her death, representatives of the other clanhouses came to the S'Och clanhouse for observance of the rituals. The shaman and the chief spoke to comfort S'Och's grieving family, though to appease S'Och's spirit they spoke of her as if she was still alive. A meal prepared by the other clanhouses was served, with the choicest food put in a serving at S'Och's accustomed eating place. After the meal this serving was burned in the hearth fire. Everyone present stayed through the night, undertaking to observe the death ways. Sleep was in relays, so that at least one member of each clanhouse was awake and in respectful attendance on the body throughout the night.

In the morning everyone able–bodied in the knat gathered by the fire at the center of the knat, grouping themselves by their clanhouses. S'Och's wrapped body was brought feet first out of the west door of her clanhouse and placed on the north side of the communal fire. After appropriate words were spoken, each member of the other clanhouses silently filed past S'Och's shrouded body, walking a great easterly circle around the fire before returning to their clanhouse's position.

The silence was nearly absolute, and tinged with apprehension. Everyone knew that S'Och's spirit was very close at this time, and could be cruel toward anyone who failed to show the proper respect.

When the clan mother of the clanhouse that Ani and Roh belonged to approached the body to begin the circle for her clanhouse, some unseemly growling could be heard coming from among the women of S'Och's clanhouse. It was not a muted vocalization of grief: it had a nasty, threatening throb to it. Everyone knew it was Okat who was making the jarring, animalistic sound.

The old, stooped clan mother stopped beside S'Och's body and looked fixedly at the women in the front row of S'Och's family. Her meaning was obvious: she was not going to let her clanhouse's part in the death walk be marred by Okat. For if Okat's growling broke the sacred concentration that was required of them, during their moments beside the body and in their walk around the circle, then the wellbeing of her entire clanhouse could be threatened. Potent shards of S'Och's spirit could remain to bedevil them, after the rest of her spirit had left for its Beyond journey. To protect her clanhouse, the clan mother was demanding that S'Och's family restore and maintain the required decorum. Okat must be made to stop her growling.

45

Among the women in the first row of S'Och's family was Ochri. Ochri was S'Och's oldest child, and Okat's older sister. She was a quiet woman. During her mother's lifetime she had always been hidden in the great shadow cast by her mother. But in the short time that had elapsed since her mother's death Ochri was emerging beautifully and gracefully into the light. She did not shrink from it, and everyone in the clanhouse could see that she had a substantial shadow of her own to cast. She did not have her mother's brusque, commanding ways, but she showed by a myriad of deft strokes that she was attune to the clanhouse's needs, and would be capable of leading it well. Some in the clanhouse with the long sight already expected that Ochri would be their next clan mother.

Ochri turned and spoke a few hushed words to the women around her; those standing behind her made way for her to go to her sister Okat. As soon as she was face to face with Okat, she began to speak in a firm whisper. Only those immediately around them could hear her words.

"You have always been our mother's favorite, Okat, and like you, I do not believe that her spirit will turn on you now, even though you provoke it mightily by this awful noise you are making. But if you persist, you will cause our mother to wander and suffer much in her journey, rather than have a straight and true path to follow. Is this how you would treat our mother, who has always sheltered you, and always without fail taken your side? And is this what you want the *rest* of the clanhouse to see and to consider? Think on this now, and tell me: Will you stop this disrespect for our mother?"

Ochri had gone to the trouble to understand her sister Okat's mind. She knew that despite their mother's lifelong love for and protection of Okat, Okat had no true regard for S'Och, or for anyone else. She knew that Okat did not care whether or not their mother would have to wander unhappily during her journey after death.

Along with everyone else in the clanhouse, she knew that her younger sister grandly aspired to be the clanhouse's next clan mother. She thought her sister's aspiration was completely unrealistic, but she also knew that as long as Okat strove to fulfill it, it had some power over her. There was probably nothing else that did.

Ochri's well–chosen words did everything that was necessary. After telling Okat before witnesses of her duty to her mother and the clanhouse, Ochri warned her that if she persisted in disrupting the ceremony, the clanhouse would not look upon what she wanted with favor.

Okat gazed back at her older sister with hatred, but she lowered her eyes and answered, "I will quiet my grieving for now," as if the disruption she'd been causing was nothing more than natural grief that she was unable to constrain.

"The clanhouse thanks you, my sister," Ochri replied in a normal tone of voice.

Okat bristled and readied an angry retort, at Ochri's presumption to speak publicly for the entire clanhouse. But Ochri had already turned away.

Ochri returned to her place and nodded once to the clan mother waiting beside S'Och's body. The death walk resumed under a fitting pall of silence.

Tears streamed down little Ani's face when it was her turn to go up to S'Och's shrouded body. Though her belly jutted out in front of her, she walked bent over and submissive. In her silent prayers she begged S'Och's spirit to be merciful toward her. S'Och had been a fruitful woman herself; Ani prayed that S'Och's spirit would understand now, with after–death enlightenment, that Ani could not possibly be blamed for the emptiness of Okat's womb.

A fitful wind bore down on the mourners, stirring up the fire in their midst and then racing away with a low moan. This wind buffeted past the clanhouses before it left the knat; some of the objects stacked alongside them could be heard tumbling or rattling around in the wind. Of course, no one left during the ceremony to investigate the wind's work; later it was found that most of the damage was minor. The contents of only one basket were ruined: it was a basket of harvested beans that Ani had hastily covered and added to a stack. When the wind toppled it, it rolled into a filth pit, where its loose cover flopped off. All of the beans inside it spilled out into the muck and were spoiled.

When it was Roh's turn to go up to his former mother–in–law's body, he walked fully upright. He was respectful, but he made no silent prayer. He reasoned that no prayer of his would make any difference at all to S'Och's spirit.

As he began to walk the circle after his moments beside the body, he suddenly felt certain that, behind him, a living S'Och had burst out of the shroud, and was swiftly coming up behind him with her long bone knife raised. The sensation was so real that he thought he could hear her approaching steps; he tensed to wheel around and face her with his own knife drawn. But in that instant, he also saw that there were no expressions of surprise or horror on the faces of the mourners as they looked past him to the north side of the circle; apparently they saw nothing unusual behind him. Sweating profusely, he forced himself to continue walking the circle. Once he rounded its southern curve he glanced anxiously at the north side where, if this was only a waking nightmare, S'Och's shrouded body would be lying bound and still on its platform. He breathed again when he saw it there, but a sharp pain sliced through his chest.

All of the members of the clanhouses walked the death walk; S'Och's family walked it last of all. The death song was sung; the sanctioned wailing began and continued while S'Och's body was carried out west of the knat. S'Och's family led the mourners and the other clanhouses followed.

Okat's wailing was the loudest and longest of all. More than once the shaman counseled her to moderate her show of grief, for the sake of her mother's spirit. Each time Okat did as he suggested for a short time, before stridently out–wailing everyone else again.

On a platform set over great pine logs, S'Och's shrouded body was placed with her feet to the west. The fire under it was lit; everyone stepped away until the fire engulfed and hid the body behind devouring sheets of white–hot flame. As the fire burned greedily the mourners approached close enough to toss dried keezhik[1] branches onto the pyre.

To complete its work the fire burned long and very hot. When the shaman signaled that the mourners could return to the knat if they wished, many left, though the shaman and some of the mourners remained until the fire completely burned down.

---

[1] cedar

The long condolence sticks from each of the other clanhouses were brought and placed carefully in front of the S'Och clanhouse. The clanhouse of S'Och's family was to remain separate from the rest of the knat, in full mourning until the tenth day after S'Och's death. During the ten–day mourning period, the other clanhouses took on many of its chores and duties, and prepared and brought food to the family inside the clanhouse, wrapped in grief.

*   *   *

After Tek's return to the knat on the sixth day of the mourning period for S'Och, his fever broke in the evening of the eighth day. He was very weak but he was made to do as much as he could for himself. One of the old women helped him get himself cleaned up, but no food or water was brought to him: he had to leave the compartment to get his sustenance for himself, and to take care of his needs.

He worked hard to regain his strength. Because of his youth he moved quickly from drinking a watery mush to eating more substantial food. Within a day he was sitting up fairly well and moving about slowly but steadily. He pushed himself further than that; he made an effort to help out with some of the lighter chores.

Everyone in the clanhouse treated him about as usual, except they were gentler since was still recovering his strength. Other than a few people that included S'Kaw, Tehwe and Tsihi, Tek did not think that they knew that he was a shapeshifter. His made–up story, about being injured far from the knat on unstable rocks, had been circulated throughout the knat, and accepted.

From the incessant talk of the clanhouse, Tek also learned everything that was generally known about S'Och's death — everything that had happened at the ceremony on the morning after her death, and of many subsequent events as well. It was all discussed solemnly, since the proper observance of the death rituals was of such importance to the wellbeing of the entire knat. The masterful words that S'Och's daughter Ochri had spoken to her sister Okat, and Okat's reply, were known to everyone: the witnesses had told others of it on their way back to the knat, after the shaman had released them from the parting ceremony. And though Roh had spoken only to his best male friend of what he had felt and thought as he walked S'Och's death circle, this was also widely known by the knat within days of the ceremony. Every gleaned detail that had, or seemed to have, any connection to the death rituals was avidly picked apart and discussed — even the fate of Ani's basket of beans.

Tek knew he was going to have to participate with everyone else in the tenth–day ceremony for S'Och. He was weak, but was no longer gravely ill.

On the morning of the tenth day he climbed shakily up the notched log to the sleeping loft to get his best clothes. They were permanently stained from the muddy drubbing that S'Kaw had given him six months earlier, but they were clean and presentable enough. A boy's finery did not have to be as nice as that of the more important people of the knat.

In the clanhouses other than that of S'Och's family, by the tenth day the grief and the fear of S'Och's spirit were lifting from the people's hearts. There was a collective feeling of relief: nearly everyone felt that the mourning had been powerful enough to appease S'Och's strong spirit. Due to their sincere and careful adherence to the strictures of the death rituals, it was reasonable to hope that their clanhouses would be safe from any disparate fragments of her spirit that might have broken away and remained among them, to cause evil.

Toward the end of the mourning period, something else dissipated the rigors of mourning for the other clanhouses. According to news seeping out of S'Och's sequestered clanhouse, serious trouble was brewing inside it. Contrary to tradition, and to all that was right and fitting, Okat was insisting that she must be chosen as her mother's replacement — as the new clan mother of her family's clanhouse.

Chapter 8

The process for choosing a new clan mother would not begin until after the parting ceremony on the tenth day of mourning. But the great void left by S'Och's death pulled everyone in her clanhouse into the fraught affair long before then. It began almost from the moment that her husband's voice was heard futilely telling S'Och that it was well past the time for her to awaken to the new day. Those within earshot were puzzled by his querulous prompting — it was something they never expected to hear. S'Och was an early riser who never had to be called to get up. But S'Och did not awaken. When her husband touched her prone body, he found that it had already cooled and stiffened. His exclamations of surprise fully roused the clanhouse, and soon afterward Okat was heard excitedly declaring that she had just awakened from a very powerful dream.

While nearly everyone struggled for composure in the first moments of grief and fearful awe of the dead, Okat insisted on telling them her dream. In it she suddenly came upon a huge bear in the forest — a bear so massive that it blocked the sun's light as it approached her. Towering above her, the bear tore its skin off and gave it to her with a low bow and pleading eyes. The moment that Okat touched the enormous pelt, she grew to be as tall as the bear, and she easily took the huge pelt into her arms. As the dream ended, before her very eyes the glistening flesh and bones of the bear's skinned carcass dulled, shrank and shriveled into the earth.

For anyone who chose to believe that Okat had actually dreamt what she so avidly described, the dream's meaning was clear: S'Och had immediately spoken from beyond death — S'Och herself had chosen Okat to be their new clan mother.

From then on Okat continually interfered with the sacred mourning time by promoting her bid to be clan mother.

51

The women of the clanhouse chose the clan mother, but everyone else, other than the infants and toddlers, were consulted for their view. Such a crucial decision intimately affected everyone. Even a mere youth might impart some essential piece of wisdom needed for the right choice.

In the ten days of mourning following S'Och's death, no one in the clanhouse was spared from Okat's relentless insistence that her bid to be clan mother must take precedence over all others. Never before had she shown the slightest interest in their cares or opinions. But in nearly every waking moment she busily promoted herself among the clanhouse's sequestered occupants. And every day she told of a new dream from the night before, signaling her exalted destiny.

These self–serving intrusions kept the clanhouse from fully immersing itself in the mourning rites, which irretrievably compromised their grieving. But no one dared to reprimand her: S'Och had always favored her in life; it was believed S'Och's potent spirit would also favor her.

They took extreme care to avoid any altercation with Okat. A mere creased brow, or doubting glance, could all too easily start an open fight with her. As long as she was the only one who was openly errant, the clanhouse hoped that none of S'Och's spirit pieces would linger and punish them with ill fortune.

Okat herself was impatient of all of the strictures for subdued behavior during the ten–day mourning period. She did not fear the dead. She was certain that the dead had no power over the living.

She knew this from her own observations, over many years. For Okat was a shapeshifter, with several animal forms. And when she was in any of her animal shapes, she could see the spirits of the dead.

She had observed them, usually at night, as they lingered before beginning their journey west. When she realized that they avoided her, she tormented them by following them in one of her two larger shapes — panther or bear, closer and closer until they broke from whatever benign purpose they had intended for their last wanderings through the knat, or the nearby forest. In this way she learned she had nothing to fear from them.

Neither did she fear that broken–off pieces of a dead person's spirit could remain behind. So many times she had looked for these shards during the ten–day mourning period after a death, and had never found any of them. Certain that they did not exist, she concluded that the dead were powerless. They were not dangerous, they did not have to be appeased, and the mourning rites were pointless.

She sometimes felt a disgruntled loneliness, because she could not share this superior knowledge with anyone else. She could not share it with her mother S'Och or the shaman, who were the only ones in the knat, other than the other shapeshifters, who knew she was a shapeshifter. Her mother was far too traditional, and she disliked the shaman too much to confide anything in him. She would not share it with another shapeshifter, because it was obvious to her that they still feared the dead — and besides she disliked them, even more than the shaman. Thus she remained alone in her true knowledge, in her fabulous uniqueness.

*   *   *

Up until the day that her husband left her, Okat had enjoyed an uncomplicated, satisfying life. She had always known that she was much smarter and better than everyone else. No one frightened her, not even the largest, most volatile men in the knat, for her mother protected her, and she knew that everyone had weaknesses that she could exploit. She honed her skills at ferreting out weaknesses, and inflicting misery. Remorse never touched her. Others in the knat had varying degrees of hard heartedness, but none of them were completely without heart, as was Okat.

Over time she built up a reputation for punishing hard and swiftly, which she was quite proud of. She never hid her skill in hurting and abasing others, except once when, as a child, she had acted with stealth. A much younger girl from another clanhouse persisted in fighting and arguing with her. She beat her with increasing severity, but nothing kept the girl down for long. Elimination was the only way to put a stop to the girl's persistent challenges to Okat's superiority, once and for all.

Young Okat had understood that elimination was different from the other punishments that she meted out. She understood that even her mother would not shield her, if it was known that she was responsible for the girl's elimination.

Preparations were not difficult: no one in the knat paid any attention to the falling outs, and making ups, among little girls. She made up with the girl, pretending to accept her as an equal, and then lured her into the forest by telling her of a spruce tree she had found, laden with large chunks of pure hardened resin. And it was a red bark spruce — the best kind for harvesting chewing resin. Together they could chip off the chunks of resin, and enjoy them just between themselves. But, Okat told her, it had to be kept secret, and they had to hurry; otherwise squirrels were bound to find it and gnaw it all away.

The girl was big and strong for her age, but her mind was too young to understand Okat's evil. Okat led her very far from the knat, close to an area that no one went to because it had sinkholes, with their chilly mists and odd sounds. Okat had no fear of the sinkholes herself, but even grown men avoided them, fearing that evil spirits lurked in their cool vapors, and would chase them on the wings of the bats that flew out of the holes in rushes of cold air.

Near one of sinkholes Okat tricked the girl into bending over, and she beat her skull in with an oak cudgel she had hidden close by. She rolled the girl's body down a slope and into a deep cold sinkhole, where it would never be found.

After that Okat grew from child to womanhood without any other serious challenge to her supremacy. Her evil took root in the knat and flourished.

Usually it was the women of the knat who suffered the most from her attacks. She had more opportunities to hurt them, since the women usually worked together on matters of growing and gathering foods. And when a man or boy was her target, she could usually hurt *him* by attacking a woman he cared about — a mother, a wife, sister, or daughter.

She expended the worst of her viciousness on the other clanhouses. This was partly because her mother S'Och had insisted early on that most of her spite be directed outside of her own clanhouse. But it was also because Okat needed her family to provide her with food and shelter, and with a favored position in the knat.

When it was time for Okat to marry, she and her mother knew better than to waste any effort on the men of the other clanhouses in the knat. Instead, they harried their own clanhouse's men into finding someone from outside the knat to marry her.

Knowing Okat's true nature, it was an unsavory task for the men. But they were all strong hunters, hardened to skillfully perform all kinds of hunts, no matter how unpleasant. They also knew that the longer it took them to bring some potential husbands to the clanhouse, the more uncomfortable their lives in it would become.

Some of them were concerned for the sake of the man who would be chosen, but they soon convinced themselves that *he* would be alright — he would not have much to lose. For if Okat treated him well, he would be the only person in the knat, besides S'Och, who was safe from her vitriol. And if she did not treat him well, then he would be free to leave. He could simply declare the marriage dissolved and leave the knat.

Before long a few likely men were brought to the clanhouse for S'Och and Okat's inspection. Roh was ultimately selected from among them.

Roh was well formed and only slightly older than the other unmarried young men in his own knat. He had felt no particular urge to marry, and had not been actively pursued by the women of his knat. His knat happened to have a surfeit of available males, and Roh was not among the more choice of them. He was easygoing and had pleasant–enough manners, but he was not very bright, and he was lazy. None of the women in his knat bothered with setting a strong enough snare for him.

But S'Och and Okat wanted him just the way he was, the better to mold and rule him, as a newcomer to their own clanhouse and knat. S'Och's commanding presence and Okat's coy enticements soon had him convinced that being single had become stale, and that marriage with Okat was going to make him very happy.

It did not make him very happy. He did not enjoy it when he realized that he had been duped into marrying a woman who was hated and feared by nearly everyone in her knat.

But Okat did treat him well: her awful ruthlessness never touched him. He also had a privileged place in the knat without having to earn it, and he did not have to work very hard. So he stayed with Okat until, after a few years of marriage, a true mating urge took hold of him, and he made his fateful decision: if he was capable of fathering children then what he wanted more than anything else was children of his own, and a wife to bear them and raise them with him. Since he and Okat remained childless, he sought elsewhere. When Ani proved capable of giving him what he wanted, he simply left Okat.

* * *

On the day that Roh left her, Okat was determined to punish both Ani and Roh immediately and spectacularly. Only one thing stopped her: she could not think of anything harsh enough — or big enough. Stymied, she shapeshifted into all three of her shapes that night, creeping from the knat in her chipmunk shape and then prowling the forest first as a bear and then as a panther. Throughout the night she roamed, thinking about her beautiful life — now ruined — and her great powers — suddenly impotent.

On her way back to the knat near daybreak she killed a small rabbit, not far from the forest's edge. It was barely old enough to be out of its birth nest. She mangled it, not really hungry enough to eat it. It was so young that its bones were still soft; its blood lacked the fuller, mature flavor that she preferred. She chomped it discontentedly one last time and was about to fling it onto the rough meadow grass when she stilled. She carried it instead to the knat's fields and laid it on one of the mounds of maize, beans and squash that Ani tended, next to the fulsome curves of a squash that was ripening despite Ani's haphazard care of its vine.

As Okat stared at the squash and the rabbit's mutilated corpse, she fleetingly glimpsed not only the best way to punish Ani and Roh, but also an entirely new existence for herself, an entirely new level of control over everyone and everything.

But no, it was unattainable. It would require such immense cunning and patience, that she knew she did not have.

She had never needed either. She had always gotten what she wanted by doing what came most naturally to her — by open, swift and violent action.

Except that one time, when she had been a girl. Then she had been cunning and patient, but she had only succeeded because it *was* so unusual. She could never transform herself from being a creature of the outright slash, to one of secret maneuverings.

Or could she?

During the rest of the summer and into the fall a curious inaction settled onto Okat; she yawed between her old, comfortable ways, and a new self she could envision, but which went against her nature, and required so much change.

Then her mother died unexpectedly, and she immediately yearned to replace her as clan mother. But here again was something that she could not possibly gain by using her old ways. Instead, cunning and patient work would be essential.

The opportunity came too soon — she had made no preparations. Still, she felt she had to try.

At the outset she did understand the likelihood of failure. But she did not understand how much an actual failure would unsettle her.

It was a great strain, caught as she was between her old self and a new, as yet ill–formed one. As the ten days of mourning crept past, she found it increasingly difficult to pretend grief she did not feel, and to follow the rituals that she thoroughly disdained.

Sometimes when she butted into yet another conversation to give another, more convincing interpretation of her latest dream, she knew her voice was too impatient and strident. She heard the discordance as the words tumbled from her mouth, and she saw subtle wincing reactions. But she could not stop herself; she always excused it as stemming from her overwrought grieving.

Something else she could not stop herself from doing was to rush at the food when it was brought in by the other clanhouses. She plucked out the choicest pieces for herself — even before the food for S'Och's place setting was selected. She told anyone nearby that what she was taking out was inferior in some way. The lies eased the anger and pressure in her slightly: she ate the best, instead of having to look at it sitting uneaten at S'Och's empty place.

In her own mind she fully excused herself for these and other lapses, born as they were of the paramount need to quickly and strongly establish her right to be the next clan mother.

*   *   *

The rest of the clanhouse warily noted the edgy volatility in Okat, and the odd attempts to dissemble that were unlike her. They redoubled their efforts not to cross her during the mourning period, and they planned among themselves to hold special rites afterward, to mend the mourning that Okat was ruining.

* * *

When no one openly contradicted Okat during the first few days of the ten–day mourning period, she began to think that she was succeeding in her bid to be clan mother. As the rest of the grim days trudged past and there was still no direct challenge, she felt a bizarre, heady confidence. Toward the end of the period, she thought that she had won over everyone for her clan mother bid — or at least built up an unbeatable number of supporters.

But she mistook silence for consent, and averted eyes for acquiescence.

* * *

Out of Okat's sight and hearing, her bid to be clan mother was quietly assessed, and firmly rejected.

It was not because she was too young, or because a clan mother was not usually a barren woman. It was because her kinswomen knew that she was irreversibly cruel and dangerous.

This was a rareness among them.

They did not understand why it was so.

But it was simply and irrefutably understood that she had always been heartlessly vicious. In the close proximity of the clanhouse, they had long seen that she had always been unsuitable, and that if she changed at all in the future then it would only be to grow worse. She was incapable of ever striving toward a good balance in life.

Countless times they had witnessed her virulent attacks on the people of the other clanhouses. Quite a few of them still remembered the girl who, many years ago, had gone into the forest with Okat and never came back. And though Okat generally sheathed her claws within her own clanhouse, every adult in it had, sooner or later, directly felt her meanness and spite — other than S'Och when she had been alive, and Roh when he had lived in the clanhouse as Okat's husband.

Now that S'Och was gone, they knew that when Okat was not given the clan mother position, some of her ire was going to be directed inward toward them, at least until they had a strong new clan mother to protect them. They did not understand the new volatility emanating from her, but they knew it did not bode well for anyone.

Independent of Okat's agitations, a viable process for choosing the next clan mother had already begun. Unlike her jarring intrusions that disrupted the mourning, it filtered quietly, tentatively through the clanhouse in brief comments and answering observations, all well within the decorum prescribed for the mourning period.

By the morning of the tenth day ceremony, Okat's eldest sister Ochri had emerged as the most likely winner.

She had not been an obvious choice at first. The clanhouse was used to S'Och's bold, openly forceful ways. Women with an outward show of strength were favored early on.

But Ochri's masterful words to Okat at the parting ceremony echoed insistently in their minds. They doubted that brute strength would have served them nearly as well as Ochri's words had in those critical moments. Unobtrusively, Ochri was examined more closely. The wiser among them already saw that though Ochri was a quiet woman, she was fully capable of wielding her mother's level of strength.

Ochri saw the support building for her. She allowed it; she encouraged it. She did so because she thought she would be a good clan mother, and because she knew she was probably the one most capable of protecting the clanhouse from the violent potential of her younger sister Okat.

Ochri was nearly twelve when Okat was born; she had been a responsible girl and had already been involved in the care of many of her clanhouse's babies and toddlers for years before Okat's birth. When she was put in charge of Okat's care, she soon noticed disturbing differences between Okat and all of the others. Okat was very quick to anger, often hitting at children twice her size, after they'd looked away. If they ran after her she hid behind her mother S'Och. S'Och and other adults laughed it off, but Ochri saw that Okat's anger was searing, and implacable. Okat also took whatever she wanted, lied about nearly everything and was an accomplished manipulator despite her young age.

While Okat was still a child, Ochri went to great lengths to impress upon her younger sister the need to conform to the ways of the People. Eventually her persistent tutelage tamed Okat, but only superficially. She knew all along that Okat was only acting. She knew that Okat was not capable of loving anyone but herself.

She had hoped that Okat would change for the better as she grew; she had seen this happen in other children who started out as mean and uncaring as Okat. But though she watched carefully for signs of a transformation, Okat was the only one who never changed for the better.

*   *   *

The men and boys of the clanhouse were usually among the best hunters in the knat. What set the very best of them apart was not brute strength and endurance, although they had plenty of that. Their edge came from their keener observation of the ways of their prey, and a fluid agility of mind to adapt to changes during the hunt.

In the clanhouse's women, similar qualities made the best leaders among them: keen powers of observation and a quickness of mind. Ochri was very well endowed with both. As she matured into womanhood and became a mother herself, she also developed a strong drive to lead and protect the people of her clanhouse from harm.

With S'Och's death, Okat became a great internal threat to the wellbeing of the clanhouse. She was increasingly volatile and might strike out at any time. She could do great harm, without any compunction. If Ochri was chosen as clan mother, she knew that one of her most important duties would be to protect the clanhouse, as well as the knat, from Okat.

Ochri did not know that her sister Okat was a shapeshifter, but she often had the uncanny thought that protecting the clanhouse from Okat would be something like hunters protecting their camp when it was being stalked by a ferocious bear or panther.

Chapter 9

The parting ceremony on the tenth day after death marked the time to restore the knat's normal rhythms. After the sequestered pause, life must go on.

During the morning and afternoon of the tenth day, all of the clanhouses were busy with preparations for the evening rites. The knat was cleaned up and swept out. Baskets, clothes, tools and weapons were sorted and put in their proper places. A great quantity of food was prepared for the communal meal. Special care was given to grooming and clothing, in keeping with the ceremony's freshening purpose.

*   *   *

The seclusion of the mourning clanhouse ended that morning. As its members began to mingle freely with the rest of the knat, Okat saw that the great sway she had built up inside the clanhouse was nothing but an illusion. Now when she intruded herself into a small group of women, instead of stilling to listen in silence, the group broke apart and melted away. And instead of averting their eyes, the women looked back at her steadily, though warily, clearly rebuffing her.

Everything she had counted on collapsed around her, and she blamed everyone else for callously leading her on, and thereby grievously shaming her. Bitterness soured her soul, and anger burned in her like a fever.

As the day wore on she also noticed the deference given to Ochri, and she accurately surmised that her boring, plodding older sister was probably going to be the next clan mother.

Her thoughts swiftly flowed through old, well–worn grooves, that demanded quick, direct and violent action. She was primed, she was ready to blaze.

In the late afternoon the large communal meal was served, with a sumptuous place setting for S'Och, one last time.

Seeking to blend in while she searched for a way to release her fury, Okat helped to serve the food. But she was hurried and sloppy: when she shoved onon at someone too quickly, gooey sauce spilt down her nicest tunic. Turning away in disgust she collided with a thin clumsy boy. Her human shape suddenly seemed inadequate to contain her outrage. Barely repressing a shape shift to panther to blindly kill, kill, kill — any and everyone — she nearly knocked the boy over as she elbowed past him.

* * *

The boy was Tek. He'd been standing too long. He was dizzy from weakness and the strong scents swirling around him, that he'd been able to smell since he'd first become a shapeshifter. When the impatient woman shoved past him he got a strong whiff of her, and about the same time he realized who she was: it was Okat. He had never been that close to her before.

* * *

The meal ended. Darkness fell, and everyone assembled around the fire at the center of the knat for the parting ceremony. The shaman spoke soothing prayers for S'Och's spirit, and an admonition against too much mourning. Then came the chanting.

The chanting urged any remaining shards of S'Och's spirit to leave, to fly off and join the main spirit on its journey west.

* * *

Listening to the chanting as she stood in the circle around the fire, Okat suddenly perceived that a perfect opportunity to punish her clanhouse had arisen. She saw a way to act decisively and violently, but also with a cunning that was still new for her.

She slipped out of the circle and hurried to the other side of the closest clanhouse, and then behind some stacked baskets. Loosening her clothes so that they would fall away from her, she shifted into her panther shape. Skirting a corner of the clanhouse, she let out a fierce and triumphant panther scream. Once around the next corner she would attack Ochri.

62

Her plan was amazingly simple: she was going to savagely maul her older sister. Then before anyone could stop her, she would escape to the forest through the entranceway in the knat's high spiked wall, which had been left open to accommodate the departure of S'Och's spirit pieces.

There was a slight risk that she'd be missed before she could slip back into the knat in her chipmunk shape, or that someone would find her hidden clothes in the meantime. But she was sure she could explain that away if she had to.

* * *

The chanting stopped the moment the blood–curdling scream rose from behind a nearby clanhouse. Some of the knaters thought it sounded like a woman's fiercely plaintive wail, but others knew exactly what it was and shouted, "Panther!" despite their great surprise, that somehow a panther was inside their knat!

Fear rippled through the crowd. If the panther could not find its own way out it was going to be very dangerous, and none of them had their weapons, other than the short bone knives they always carried. The weapons they really needed were out of reach — they had been put away during the preparations for the ceremony, stacked or hung inside their clanhouses.

"Find it! Find where it is!" the hunters shouted.

They did not have to look long or far. The panther roared and screamed again as it approached the circle, which hastily parted where the panther was closest. The panther stepped fully into the light of the fire, already walking in a crouch toward where Ochri was backing away with two other women.

Some of the hunters filtered through the crowd and put themselves between the panther and the three women, while others rushed to get their weapons. The hunters in front of the panther shouted and waved their short knives; Okat as the panther quickly transferred her pent up malice from Ochri to them, her primal mind reacting lightning fast. She could use patience and cunning against Ochri later on. Right now she had a short time, before escaping, to lunge at one of the hunters. None of them knew she was not an ordinary panther; none knew that she was not at all confused by their

63

shouting, by their waving arms, or by their feinting and jabbing with their short knives.

Okat quickly chose her victim: Tek's brother Sho. She leapt at the hunter next to him, and in the last second she twisted in the air toward him, poised to sink her teeth into his neck and rip his belly open with her claws.

Seemingly from out of nowhere a snarling wolf lunged at the panther, a tiny owl and a huge hawk dove at it from the dark sky, and a thin crazed buck rushed in to flail at it with its hooves.

In the melee of fang, feather and hoof Okat missed her target and sprang away from the fire, into the cover of darkness. The wolf, birds and buck swiftly followed, harrying her as she fled. Fully armed hunters joined the chase, others brought torches; they followed the three four–legged animals, taking different paths between the clanhouses to corner them, or to get a good shot at them. Despite the confusion, they soon realized that the three running animals, with the panther in the lead, were heading toward the knat's entranceway.

Shouts, hoarse with kill lust, filled the air. All of the hunters were after the panther, but many pursued the other animals as well — rushing away from the fire to get their weapons, they had not seen the wolf, birds and buck attack the panther. All of the animals sensed the danger and moved rapidly, erratically through the darkness.

Some of the hunters worked to slow the animals down by waving torches at them and rushing them; others raced to block the entranceway. None had gotten in a good shot yet: in the twists and turns among the clanhouses there was too great a chance of hitting another hunter, or a panicked child or woman.

When Okat reached the entranceway, three hunters already blocked it. One of them was her former husband Roh. She immediately charged, certain that Roh would flinch and she would get past him. She planned to take a swipe at him too as she escaped.

But the shaman stepped out from behind the three hunters and faced the charging panther with his arms raised. "Stop! Everyone!" he shouted, while staring directly at Okat and shaking his turtle–shell rattle at her.

The shaman was old and many thought he was far past his prime, but at that moment in the flickering torchlight, there was something terrible and commanding about him. Everyone obeyed him, except Okat. She complied only because she had no other choice.

The shaman had some power over her. She was forced to slow to a stop before him. She could not pass him, or go another way. She did not know what this power was, but she guessed it was from something he was wearing, or the rattle he was pointing at her.

The noise and shouting of the chase abruptly quieted. The shaman spoke gravely, never letting his stern gaze leave the dangerous panther. He told the hunters to lower their weapons, and he had the three hunters who were behind him, swing around to his side and join the others.

Then he barked, "Owl. Hawk. Go." Without hesitation the owl and the hawk rose up from where they had perched and banked away into the darkness. The wolf and buck remained near the knat's wall, close behind the panther.

The shaman told everyone to come closer to hear him, though he warned them to keep a distance from himself and the three wild animals.

Quickly, quietly word passed back through the knat. While the stragglers were arriving, the shaman feverishly wracked his brain, trying to decide what he was actually going to say to them all.

He knew that Okat as the panther had ruined the end of the tenth day ceremony for her mother S'Och, and that she would have mauled or killed someone if the four other shapeshifters had not risked exposure and their lives to prevent it. He knew that the lives of Okat and the wolf and buck shapeshifters now depended entirely on him. He was angrier with Okat and more shocked by her than he had ever been, but he saw that tradition did not permit him to let the hunters kill her here. She was still one of the People, and she had not actually mauled or killed anyone this night.

More expediently, he could not think of a way to convince the hunters to take down the panther while sparing the wolf and the buck. He was a hunter himself and fully understood the kill lust. Now, here — palpable. The hunters did not know the secret of the shapeshifters, and many of them would not differentiate among killing panther, wolf or buck. If he could not persuade the hunters to let all three shapeshifters go free, then they would all die here.

He must prevent the death of the wolf and buck shapeshifters if he could. To do that, he would have to allow Okat escape along with them. And she was going to have to go first because she was not immobile. She paced a long ellipse in front of him. He could see in her eyes that the other two shapeshifters would never get past her.

The secrets of the shapeshifters was not something the shaman could speak of to the rest of the knaters. He continued to cast about in his mind for something he could tell the knaters when they had all gathered. It was hard for him, because he was not very imaginative. But something had to be said, that would suffice.

"Sometimes," he told them when he at last began to speak, "the animals of the forest mourn our greatest losses as much as we do ourselves. Perhaps, sometimes, even more so. We are not blessed to know why this is so. But as your shaman I have learned that it . . . is . . . sometimes so.

"This evening as our formal mourning for S'Och was ending, five forest animals — two of the birds and three of those that walk on four legs — came silently into our knat and our circle to mourn with us. Normally of course they would never enter our knat, but these in their grief could not help themselves. They could not stay away.

"One of them could not moderate its grief as we do, as we have all been taught to do. This one — this panther — let its grief overwhelm it, and it went berserk in our midst. Then the others that came to mourn with us — the owl and the hawk, the wolf and the buck — these four sought to protect us from the wildness of their sister, the panther.

"They did this until I was able to use power from S'Och's spirit to stop the panther. It is under this power now, and it will stay under this power until I permit it to return to the forest. I have already let the owl and the hawk go. The wolf and the buck wait for my permission to leave our knat, unhindered. Unharmed."

The shaman paused, to let his words sink in. The panther had stopped pacing, and the knaters looked with surprise and uncertainty at the panther, wolf and buck. Nothing in their experience prepared them for this strange and unprecedented ending to S'Och's tenth day ceremony.

The age–old fear was that when any wild forest animal walked in a knat of the People, it was because the animal was possessed by an evil spirit — a slobberer. It came alone with eyes glazed and a foamy saliva dripping from its muzzle. It wandered erratically, and sometimes it attacked. Inevitably it was felled by a hunter's spear or arrow, and its fallen body was treated as unclean, because of the evil spirit that had possessed it.

But just now there had been five wild creatures in their knat, all at the same time, and right at the end of S'Och's ceremony. Two of them had left, exactly as the shaman had directed them to do. And the three that were still here — the three four–legged ones — they stood before the knat's shaman, very much as if they were attending to what he was saying.

An animal inhabited by a slobberer could not possibly do this! And all of these oddities could not be coincidences — they had to be mystical. In a thrall of wonder the people put their faith in their shaman; they allowed themselves to be guided by him.

"The panther will leave first," the shaman announced, and the knaters watched to see if the panther, so oddly still now, would do as the shaman directed. The hunters among them gripped their weapons tightly, partly in readiness to protect their shaman if necessary, but also because they all coveted the panther's gorgeous pelt. Even in the dim light cast by flaming pine knots and a rising quarter moon, the panther's luxuriant fur dazzled their eyes.

* * *

The panther's cold, blank gaze swept the assembled knaters, seeing every one of them much more clearly than they saw it.

Okat as the panther registered the desire for her pelt in the hunters' eyes, but this did not stoke her anger now. She had long since recovered from her pique of frustration. The virtues of patience and cunning ascended once more in her firmament. She only wanted a way out, and the shaman was giving her one. She would do as he directed, for the time being.

* * *

The shaman stepped well aside so that the panther had a clear path to the knat's entranceway. As Okat passed him in her panther form he worked to increase the power he had over her, just in case she tried extra hard in these crucial moments to break free of it.

67

* * *

Okat saw him shake the rattle in his left hand several times, and guessed that his power over her resided in it. Her panther face remained blank, but she growled nastily in her throat as she passed out of the knat.

A fading vestige of her anger made her want to lay in wait for the wolf and the buck, but the power over her compelled her to race away to the forest instead.

* * *

The shaman moved closer to the entranceway and signaled, with casual authority, for the wolf to leave next. The wolf walked toward the entranceway with a fearless stride and no hint of aggression. Its ears were forward and its tail curled up.

Again the hunters gripped their weapons tighter, but this time they had no fear for their shaman. It was only because another fine pelt was walking out of range and away. It was not nearly as nice as the panther's, but was still well worth having.

Like Okat, the young man who had shapeshifted into a wolf knew what the hunters were thinking. He left the knat with hackles raised and lips rippling back in a proud snarl. As he passed close to the shaman, the shaman raised his arms slowly and spoke over it, telling it to continue to mourn through the night, but that early in the new day, it should rest in a certain hemlock grove, and then take up its normal life again.

* * *

Tek as the buck had stood very still in the shadows ever since the shaman and the huge bear shapeshifter blocked the panther's way. He could barely stand, and was afraid at times that he was going to collapse.

A breeze buffeting through the entranceway carried scents from there toward Tek, and he realized that the bear shapeshifter had no scent at all. It only took him a moment longer to realize that the bear was not a shapeshifter, and that it could not be an ordinary bear either. As a deer shapeshifter he knew that everything in the world had its own distinct scent, and in this moment every scent drifting toward him from the entranceway had a scent, except the bear.

Earlier, when he had seen and smelled the panther as it approached the circle, he knew it was Okat, and that she meant to do serious harm. Hunters were yelling back and forth; some were saying they had the panther covered; others yelled they'd get their spears and bows. Still very weak from his illness, Tek ran as fast as he could to get his own weapons. But before he got very far, a small owl flew over his head going toward where Okat was as panther. Tsihi! She was so small, so slight — he turned back, to protect her no matter what. He could not do it as a weakened boy; he would have more strength as a buck. He slipped out of sight, shapeshifted and followed Tsihi. When nearly there he saw that the big hawk was already there and was blocking Tsihi from diving at Okat. As he watched Tsihi broke free and dove toward Okat, with the hawk close behind.

Tek got a clear view of the panther lunging at the hunter beside his brother Sho. But he knew from instinct, as had Tsihi, that Okat's real target was Sho. Before he could get there to beat at Okat with his sharp hooves, a wolf lunged in, and the hawk hurled itself at Okat right behind Tsihi. Tek joined the fray, though his buck nerves jumped from being so close to the wolf, the panther, and the hunters crowding them. He was surrounded by so many of a buck's natural enemies.

When Okat broke and ran Tek followed her closely with the others, though his breathing was ragged and he staggered several times. Weakness from his illness affected him, even in his buck form.

When the shaman and the large bear stopped Okat, Tek stilled and tried to recover some of his strength. Though bears were also a natural enemy of a buck, Tek didn't even wonder about it. And he barely noticed that the wolf was eyeing him now and again, as the shaman arranged for their escape. Tek knew from the wolf's scent that he was a shapeshifter too — he was one of the young men from a clanhouse near the S'Och clanhouse. He didn't know them very well, though, so he wasn't sure which young man it was.

When it was Tek's turn to leave the knat, he mustered enough strength to walk toward the shaman and the bear with his head up, though his breathing was still labored and gulping.

* * *

69

The hunters' hands again flexed on their weapons, but now it was from habit. The buck was too thin for its meat to be any good, and its pelt hung too loose and looked mangy. That together with its audible wheezing . . . it could well have a wasting illness. Despite its rather well–formed antlers, this was a buck that they would probably pass on in the forest. They were not tempted to fell it now.

* * *

As Tek got closer to the entranceway where the shaman and the bear waited for him, he stopped and stared at the bear. It seemed to Tek that it was growing larger. Its heavy fur lifted in a wind that came up and whirled around it. The air seemed to throb with a power emanating from it. Tek then understood that this bear was an extremely powerful spirit.

He bowed low before it. Though he had little strength left he knelt on both of his front legs. He arched his neck and bent it down until the front tips of his antlers touched the ground. The throbbing in the air around the bear became more like waves rolling outward from it. To Tek it felt like the waves were washing over him, and then through him. He felt strength returning, but it had a different quality to it. It seemed to Tek that this strength was something deeper, and more spiritual, than physical strength.

The feeling of waves passing through him ended; the throbs dissipated; all became still again. He raised his head. The bear was no longer there; it had vanished. He got up and approached the shaman.

The shaman looked at him quizzically, and then at the rattle in his left hand.

As Tek passed the shaman, he spoke the same words that he had spoken to the wolf. Tek thought he understood the shaman's message: before morning, someone was going to leave clothes for him and the wolf shapeshifter in that small grove of hemlock trees. Once they retrieved their clothes, they would be able to return unobtrusively to the knat.

As a buck Tek did not feel safe from any wolf, shapeshifter or not. He resolved that when morning came, he would stay downwind of the grove until he was sure that the wolf shapeshifter had gotten his clothes and left.

Once he was outside the knat, he sniffed for the scent trail of the panther and wolf, and went away in a different direction than they had. On alert for all kinds of danger, including that either the panther or the wolf had changed course to waylay him, Tek headed for the part of the forest where he had most often gone, when he had been troubled by the dreams that preceded his first shapeshifting.

*   *   *

The knat entranceway was lashed shut for the night. The shaman gave a brief final prayer for S'Och's spirit, and then dispersed everyone to their clanhouses.

While the knat was quieting down the shaman went first to the clanhouse where the young man Woq lived. Woq's older brother met with the shaman there. He was one of the very few that knew his brother Woq was a wolf shapeshifter. He had already retrieved Woq's clothes from where Woq had shed them, before shapeshifting into a wolf, and he had prepared a bundle of Woq's everyday clothes for the shaman. The shaman took the bundle and proceeded to the S'Kaw clanhouse, where he was informed by Tsihi that everything had been retrieved. Tsihi gave the shaman a bundle of Tek's everyday clothes.

The shaman returned to his own clanhouse with the two bundles, tired and brooding over the harm that could be done by a vindictive woman who cared for no one but herself. Okat had always been a brazen liar and insufferably conceited. She had been bad for the knat her entire life, but had become markedly worse when she began to shapeshift. From then on, she had no respect for the sacred ways of the People. The shaman's small influence over her had evaporated.

Now that her mother S'Och was dead, no one had any power over Okat, and she was sure to get worse than ever. She was becoming like a terrible force of nature in their midst. He no longer thought of her as a fitting member of the knat.

He sat on the stump beside his living compartment, fingering the rattle that had stopped Okat in her tracks.

He had been shaking it as usual during the chanting earlier that evening. But when Okat as the panther screeched her blood–curdling scream, the rattle took on a life of its own. It raised very high, yanking him up off his toes, and then it swung down so low that he fell with it to his hands and knees. When he scrambled up, he tried to let go of the rattle but couldn't: it was as if a great strong hand was clenched over his.

When the panther approached the circle the rattle rose and pointed directly at it, shaking in a rapid blur like the tip of a rattlesnake's tail. But the sound of the rattle was lost in the hubbub, and the panther completely ignored it.

Hunters with short knives ran past the shaman and yelled for everyone to stay back behind them. The rattle in the shaman's hand went limp again, until the panther began to run among the clanhouses. Then the rattle yanked the shaman to go with it, but not in the direction that the panther had run. Stumbling and tripping as he was pulled and yanked along by the rattle, the shaman ended up nearly breathless in the narrow passage of the knat's entranceway, where it curved for a short distance along the outside wall. Soon afterward three hunters ran up, to kill the wild animals if they tried to escape through the entranceway. The rattle led the shaman past these hunters, where he confronted Okat and held her in check with the rattle's power.

Never before had the shaman held anything in his hand with that kind of power, and he never wanted to again. The power had used him as its vessel, without his consent. He was nothing more than a useful tool to it, rather than who he really was — a deeply spiritual man. He felt demeaned by it.

And he feared it was a malevolent vestige of the deceased S'Och's spirit — the very spirit that they all had been trying to assuage with the mourning rites.

And yet, the shaman mused, he was not certain about that. The boy Tek as a buck had bowed low to the rattle, and when he got up there was a difference about him, though the shaman could not say just what it was. He did not think that Tek would have bowed like that, and looked like that when he got up, if the rattle's power was an evil force . . .

He wondered if some of the power in the rattle had moved to the boy. Well, whether it had or not, it was certain that there was no longer any power in the rattle. It was an ordinary rattle, inert.

The shaman put it away and called to one of his daughters. In private he gave her the two bundles of clothes and asked her to quietly take them to the knat wall where it ran closest to their clanhouse. When she was sure that no one was watching, she was to throw both of the bundles over the wall there.

* * *

The shaman's daughter did as she was told. When the bundles landed outside the wall, Woq came forward silently and picked them both up. He put on his own clothes, and carried the bundle of Tek's clothes away.

Chapter 10

Tek reached his favorite tree safely. There he changed back into a boy and climbed shakily into the tree. It was the safest place he could think of to spend the night.

The top of this tree must have been loped off long ago, perhaps as a sapling. After a length of thick trunk, five massive branches curved outward and upward, something like the rigid ribs of a round basket. Tek settled into the irregular hollow where the branches began their upward curve, and fell asleep almost immediately. He slept deeply until a dream of wolves chasing him startled him awake.

He smelled wolf very close by, the moment he awoke. It was not an ordinary wolf though . . . it had the scent of the wolf shapeshifter, and it was . . . in the tree with him!

Tek recoiled, instantly awake and backing away between two of the huge branches. He readied himself to jump down to the ground, only pausing, tensed, to learn which way the wolf would spring at him.

"Don't be stupid," a gruff, disgusted voice said to him from the darkness of the other side of the hollow. "I'm not going to eat you. At least not now. I'm full, and besides there's hardly any meat on you. I'm Woq. Here — your clothes." A bundle of clothes hit Tek in his chest.

Woq talked while Tek got dressed. And continued to talk. And then talked some more.

As the last of the night passed and the grey of first light filtered through the pine needles of their bower, Tek barely had a chance to say anything. Even when Woq asked Tek a question, he usually answered it himself before Tek had a chance to speak. Tek supposed that Woq talked a lot in the privacy of his own clanhouse. Or maybe his tongue was loosened simply because they were both shapeshifters. Though that connection was clearly going to have its limits.

"A while ago when the shaman told me we had a buck shapeshifter among us — of course he didn't say who it was but shapeshifters find each other. I knew it had to be you — it's so strange that you're a buck. What good is a buck shapeshifter? We hunt deer, we eat deer. Deer are prey. So it has to be a huge mistake — because how can you hunt yourself? You can't of course. That would be like killing yourself to eat your own arm or leg. So it's strange, very strange. It's like you'll always be your own worst enemy — or something like that.

"And you'll never be safe from the rest of us. I mean, I suppose I'll try not to eat you when you're a buck and I'm a wolf, especially since the shaman told me not to. But it'll be hard. It's so unnatural.

"Unless — can you turn into anything else besides a buck? Something better — like a wolf? Probably not — if you could've you'd have done it last night. So buck's your only shape."

Woq paused for breath, and Tek quickly asked him how he had found him. That had really been worrying him.

"Easy! Well, maybe not so easy for some, but easy for me. I already knew you've been coming to this area, and to this tree. I've got a wolf shapeshifter's keen sense of smell, like your buck's. For a long time I could smell that you'd been here, and I saw you here a few times, sitting near this tree. I wondered about it. Were you just being lazy? No, you looked too bothered about something for that. Moping over some girl? That wasn't really like you either. Besides, it's obvious that all the good ones have been taken. Your brother — anyway I knew you came here a lot, and I got your scent last night while you were a buck, and put it together. Where else would you go but here? Easy.

"You're new to this, aren't you? I could tell you a few things about it, I guess, even though the shaman's going to teach you. Except that there are some things about us shapeshifters that the shaman doesn't know. Like, we can see the spirits of the dead when we're animal. You can too, right? Or maybe you haven't had a chance to yet — but you will. See, the shaman doesn't know about that. None of us have told him. Okat would never tell him because she hates him. The rest of us — Tsihi, S'Kaw and me — we don't like talking about it, even to each other. It just feels secret, you know? Yes, I think you know."

"Anyway, my animal shape is wolf and I've had it for about two years now. Tsihi's is owl and she's had it for about as long — maybe a little longer. I've only seen S'Kaw as hawk, but the shaman once told me he thinks she might have another shape — I don't know how long she's been a shapeshifter but probably a really long time — like from when she was about our age. That's about when it starts.

"But just because we're all shapeshifters doesn't mean we get along, or were meant to get along. And you're so different because you're, you're prey — I really don't see how you'll ever fit in.

"Anyway, S'Kaw's not at all friendly with me even though we share this shapeshifting. She doesn't get along with you either, right? Well, that's not going to change now, especially since your only shape's a buck. What could a buck ever have in common with a hawk?

"S'Kaw's a deep one. And she's got a real mean streak — at least that's what I think. Tsihi says her grandmother always has a good reason when she's mean, that it's always for the best. Of course, Tsihi would get along well with her own grandmother — most granddaughters do. And the rest of S'Kaw's family does seem to respect her . . .

"I get along well with Tsihi. We grew up together and Tsihi is . . . Tsihi is sweet like the plumpest blackberries . . . except she's a bird. If your brother hadn't — but it might not have worked out — I mean a wolf and an owl . . . if we'd married, I might have . . . and her feathers would . . . no, it wouldn't have worked. And besides her grandmother S'Kaw was set against it. It was never even discussed but I could tell — the S'Kaw stare. No words necessary, you know? Oh, yes, you'd know.

"Then there's Okat." Woq had been talking faster and faster until he got to Okat. He stopped abruptly and seemed to be thinking hard about something. Tek had some questions but he could see this wasn't the right time to speak.

Woq started up again, speaking slowly. "Okat can be so cruel. The pain she causes — she enjoys it. It's like food to her. And for some reason that we don't understand — I mean that the rest of us shapeshifters and the shaman, we don't understand — Okat is the one of us who has the most shapes. The shaman says she has three — the panther you saw, a smallish black bear, and another one that's either real small or winged — the shaman doesn't know what it is yet. She uses it, you see, to secretly get in and out of the knat at night when the entranceway is lashed shut.

"It's so unfair. Okat is so dangerous. Even before she was a shapeshifter, when she was young . . . do you already know about the girl that went into the forest with Okat and didn't come back?"

This time Woq didn't go on to answer the question for Tek, so Tek said that yes, he'd heard about it. "What clanhouse was she from?" Tek asked, though looking at Woq he thought he could guess which one it was.

Though Tek's guess was not spoken, Woq nodded. "My clanhouse. Her name was Woqri. She was my sister, born at the same time as me.

"That's why I was so disappointed when I found out that you were only a buck. A buck can't — I'd been hoping for . . .

"Woqri and I were both so alike — we were very wild when we were little. We fought with everybody, to show how tough we were. I fought other boys; Woqri usually fought with girls of course, but not always. Well, some of the older boys beat some sense into me. Then I didn't fight as much. But with Woqri, the fighting was mostly always with Okat. Okat was older than Woqri and me but Woqri was almost as big and strong as Okat.

"Woqri came to me one afternoon, all beat up and bloodied from another fight with Okat, and she told me that she wasn't going to fight Okat anymore, no matter what. She said . . . she said that Okat wasn't a person. She said Okat was a thing, like the lightning in a thunderstorm. It was odd. I thought she was muddled up from getting hit in the head too hard.

"Then they seemed to make up. A few days after that, they went into the forest together, and Woqri never came out of it.

"Okat killed my sister. I know this in my heart. She must have planned it, and then tricked her somehow. Okat would never have been able to kill Woqri in a fair fight.

"When Okat came back to the knat alone, she said that she and Woqri had gone berry picking, in one of those clearings in the forest. Okat said that Woqri just went off alone into the forest, and wouldn't come back with her. Okat made it sound like whatever had happened to Woqri was Woqri's own fault.

"I remember the next day like it was yesterday — a group of us went with Okat to where she said they'd been berry picking. S'Kaw was one of the women in the group of us. When we got there everyone was moving around, looking to see if they could find Woqri, or signs of which way she'd gone. And I remember seeing S'Kaw moving around but stopping now and again with her head back and eyes half closed. I didn't understand then what she was doing, but I noticed it. And I noticed the way she looked at Okat, when Okat was repeating her tale about her and Woqri picking berries there, and then Woqri wandering off. S'Kaw looked . . . really upset. S'Kaw's so secretive, but I'd been watching her, and I could tell.

"A few years ago, when I became a shapeshifter, one of the best parts about it was the keen sense of smell. Then the shaman told me that S'Kaw was a shapeshifter too, though I'd guessed that on my own. Anyway, I remembered back to that day at the berry place, and I knew that S'Kaw had been trying to get my sister's scent, so that she could follow it and find her.

"But she could not find Woqri's scent there. I knew that, once I was a shapeshifter myself, and thought back to what I'd seen her do. Now, a hawk doesn't have a keen sense of smell, so S'Kaw's other shape must be something that does. Anyway, from the way that S'Kaw looked at Okat, I knew that Okat had to be lying about her and Woqri being at the berry place together.

"We searched everywhere for Woqri. The women searched in the areas closer to the knat; the men and boys went far into the forest and a long way up and down the river. And they asked about her at the other knats, for a great distance. No one knew anything.

"I miss my sister Woqri. I think about her every single day. And every day I try to learn one more thing that will help me get at Okat, for killing my sister. Every day I ask myself if I have found the way yet. So far, I haven't. Okat is . . . so dangerous, and she's getting worse. You saw — last night — she's never done anything like *that* before. So unexpected . . . she was — no mistaking that panther scream, that roar. She was going for blood. I went to wolf without thinking — I don't usually do that — against something like a panther, wolves have to work together with other wolves. But there was no time to plan anything. And together our reaction — the four of us did manage to — but you could see that even working together we were not nearly strong enough to kill her. You and the birds helped a little — you distracted her, rattled her. With that and the hunters chasing us — she tried but she never was able to close on me, during that wild run through the knat.

"Then the shaman *had* to let her go — to save us, you see? He had some kind of hold over her, but it must not have been strong enough to hold her while we got past her. At least that's what I think. I know the shaman fairly well, better than most. I can usually tell when he's not sure about something. It's not all that easy for him, being a shaman.

"I need at least one other wolf. My sister Woqri — she would have been a wolf just like me. A strong and fierce one. I am certain of it. Together we might have — but she's gone. Dead." Woq looked at Tek appraisingly. "You'll let me know if you get the wolf shape, or something else that would be useful? Yes, you will."

They — mainly Woq — talked for a little while longer. Tek was able to get answers to some of his questions. Among other things Woq mentioned that Okat was probably already back in the knat. She'd use her third shape — the one they hadn't identified yet — to get back in. But overall Woq had lost interest in talking with Tek. Tek knew what Woq was thinking: to Woq, Tek was just a skinny boy who wouldn't be of any use to him in avenging his sister's death, either as a boy or as a buck.

Tek thought about asking Woq whether he had seen the bear that stood beside the shaman, but he didn't. Woq was right: there were some things a shapeshifter wouldn't normally talk about, even with another shapeshifter. Seeing the bear — it seemed very private and personal to Tek, as did seeing S'Och's spirit after her death.

Tek and Woq left the tree, split up and returned to the knat.

* * *

As Woq predicted, Okat returned to the knat long before he and Tek did. A few hours before dawn she crept up beside the knat wall, listening to make sure all within was quiet. To get inside, she shapeshifted into her human shape, and then through to her chipmunk shape. Her clothes were where she had left them; she shapeshifted from chipmunk to human and moved her clothes to a basket outside her own clanhouse, where she would retrieve them in the morning. Shapeshifting back into a chipmunk, she entered the clanhouse through a crevice in the layers of bark. She easily slipped into her own compartment without being detected.

Chapter 11

When Tek got back to the knat that morning he was still looking forward to talking with Tsihi about shapeshifting. But he soon realized that she was avoiding him. Then S'Kaw's husband Tehwe took him aside, and told him to come to him if he needed any help with 'that deer problem'. While Tehwe was telling Tek this, his manner was unenthusiastic and distant. Tek understood that he should not try to talk with Tsihi about it, and that he should only ask for help if he had no other choice.

* * *

It was the shaman who instructed Tek about shapeshifters. Instruction was not lengthy.

No one knew why some of the People had this ability, and no one knew if it was for good, or for evil. Some thought that shapeshifting corrupted the person, sooner or later, and inevitably led to evil. The shaman himself thought that it depended on the person. It was just . . . unfortunate that in the old stories about shapeshifters, they were usually evil, or at least seriously flawed. Because of these . . . concerns, and because it was an unnatural ability, it was wise for a shapeshifter to keep it secret. Usually only the shaman and a close relative of the shapeshifter knew — other than other shapeshifters in the knat who had, in an animal form, a keen sense of smell..

When in their animal forms the shapeshifters still had a vestige of their human scent. Thus it was easy for a shapeshifter with a keen sense of smell to distinguish among the scents of the people in their knat. When they came across the scent of a person in an animal, they connected that animal with the person, and knew.

Normally there was at most one shapeshifter in a knat, even in larger knats. Often they were shamans. The Ochwah knat was unusual in having five shapeshifters; the shaman thought it was because of the knat's history. Much more so than other knats, it was a mix of several disparate knats that had combined. Tek, as the fifth shapeshifter, had himself come from another knat.

Most shapeshifters were predators in their animal form. This seemed to be in harmony with the People being great hunters. The shaman didn't know what to make of Tek being a buck; he had never heard of anyone who shapeshifted into a deer. He was curious about whether Tek could eat meat when he was a person, and, more importantly, whether he was going to be able to hunt deer for the knat. Tek admitted that he avoided eating deer meat now, though he could still eat the meat of other animals. He could still fish and hunt small game. He didn't know if he was ever going to be able to kill a deer.

The shaman asked Tek why he had made that low bow to his rattle, on the night that S'Och's mourning ended. Tek did not want to tell the shaman about the bear, so he just said he didn't know why he did it. The shaman did not believe him, but after glaring at him he asked him no more questions about it.

The shaman knew that the shapeshifters were not telling him everything. He was closest to Woq; they talked often — or more accurately, Woq talked and the shaman listened. Sometimes Woq admitted something without meaning to, giving the shaman an insight. But even Woq tried to be cautious about what he said to the shaman.

The shaman urged Tek to come to him and tell him of any new developments. There might be something the shaman could do — if necessary, he could perform a special ceremony, or perhaps seek a sign from the great spirits. But, he admonished with some sourness, there was nothing he could do if a shapeshifter did not confide in him.

Tek asked the shaman if he could just stop being a shapeshifter. The shaman's reply was that he didn't think so; he thought that Tek would be a shapeshifter for the rest of this life.

He told Tek that he must shapeshift into a buck often enough, but that only Tek would know how often that was. Otherwise, a discordance was bound to build up inside him, and come out in an unusual way, at an inconvenient time.

And of course, because Tek's shape was a buck, he must always avoid hunters.

* * *

Tek did not want to shapeshift into a buck any more often than he had to, even though there were some wonderful things about it — like the feeling of being perfectly intended for life in the forest, and the peace of living richly and simply there — at least, when he was certain he was far from predators.

But Woq was right. Being a buck put him at odds with being one of the People, and Tek wanted more than anything else to be an ordinary boy of his clanhouse and knat.

Tek put shapeshifting out of his mind and concentrated on just being Tek, of the People. He worked in earnest to regain all of his strength, pushing himself to do the harder chores. He gathered more of the larger branches and logs for the hearth fires. He lifted heavier loads. He ran whenever he could, instead of walking.

When the boys were called together to open up some of the forest for new planting fields, Tek worked as long and as hard as he could with the rest of them. Under the guidance of the old men, the boys hacked out the brush, and dragged and stacked it for rough fencing. Then, with acorns and other tree fruits bouncing off their heads and shoulders, they girded the trees. A girded tree would not leaf out next spring, giving the new plantings full sun.

As they worked the boys' talk was of hard winters, and of the fall raids that the men were planning.

The old men had predicted that the coming winter would be a harsh one, with heavy snows and frigid bear winds. The boys could not know as much about forecasting the winter as the old men did; they contented themselves with vying half–heartedly to relate the worst of the snows and cold they had known.

But the really avid talk was about the upcoming raids.

Over the summer the men went from knat to knat, for formal meetings, visiting and trading. Much of it was beneficent, but inevitably there were disagreements — some new ones, others older and festering. Some were minor; others cut deep. By summer's end the men of the Ochwah knat talked seriously among themselves about which wrongs ought to be redressed by raiding, and the relative strengths and weaknesses of the other knats.

Fall was the time for raiding. In peaceful times like the present, raiding kept the warrior skills honed, and it trained up the younger men.

A few of the bigger, stronger boys would be chosen to go on the raids with the men. There was much talk among the boys about who would be picked, and of the feats in past raids and the periodic wars. Tek mostly listened, since he was still fairly new to the knat. He didn't want to be chosen, but even if he had wanted it, he knew he'd be passed over. Though he had more strength every day, he was still thin, and it was a struggle for him to do his full share of the work.

By evening he was worn out from his days' strengthening exertions. As soon as he ate he went to the loft to sleep, until one day he noticed that Tsihi was upset about something. He hung around to watch and listen, and soon knew all about it: his brother Sho was going on the upcoming raids, and Tsihi did not want him to go. This surprised him at first: surely she understood that this was something her husband had to do.

But her irritation made more sense to him when he overheard the women talking, and found out that Tsihi was pregnant. Her belly had not swollen yet, but her unreasonableness had something to do with the changes that happened to an expectant mother.

That was about when Tek began to notice a difference in Tsihi's scent, and that there was the same difference in the scent that drifted from the other expectant women. Within another day or so Tek became aware of more differences in the scents of all of the women. And some of the women exuded something in their scent that made Tek *feel* that he should compete with all of the other males to impress and please them; except that Tek's *mind* told him that it would be ridiculous for him to even try it. His mind roiled confusedly with this strengthening feeling.

Then with sudden insight Tek understood what was happening to him. Bucks rutted in the fall, fighting each other and chasing the does to mate with them. For a month or so they were so distracted by the rut that they were much easier to hunt. Because he was a deer shapeshifter, Tek was affected by the fall rut, and he realized that the weird feeling was going to get stronger. He decided that it would be

84

much better to get through the rut as a buck in the forest, rather than as a scent–addled boy in the knat.

He went to Tehwe, and then to the shaman, telling them that he was going to have to go into the forest for a while, and would come back as soon as he could. The smell of the women, he told them, was driving him crazy. His manner was assertive, even combative, though he had not intended to behave that way toward the older men.

After absorbing Tek's manner and what he was saying, both men readily agreed that he should go. They counseled him to go as high up into the mountains as he could, but Tek already knew that. There were plenty of deer in the valleys in the fall, so hunters rarely went very high into the hills.

Neither Tehwe nor the shaman knew how to explain his absence, but they assured him that they would think of something.

Tek left the knat with his short bow. He stashed his clothes and the bow in a carefully selected tree crotch, and for nearly a month he was a buck wandering the high hills and mountains far away from the knat. He resisted the urge, sometimes quite strong, to descend to the lower lands to find some bucks to fight with. Instead, he scraped his antlers on trees incessantly and marked everywhere, though it attracted neither does for mating nor other bucks for fighting. When he did occasionally come across a doe, she ran from him. If he followed her and got too close, she would wheel on him, raise herself up on her hind legs and beat with her front hooves to keep him away. Tek supposed that his boy scent was repellent to the does. He didn't really mind, because whenever he got close enough to the doe, he always found that there was something indefinably wrong about her scent anyway.

There were no hunters, and Tek stayed clear of bears, wolves and panthers. He could scent them from a great distance and knew their ways. He always crossed some streams and slipped around downwind and far from them. They didn't pursue him; Tek wondered if his shapeshifter scent seemed wrong to them as well. Or maybe it was just because other prey was so plentiful in the fall.

The mountain air got colder; more and more often his breath misted on still mornings. With the cold driving the sap from the tips of the bushes, his forage was less succulent.

When the wildness of the rut finally eased in him, he was two mountains away from the knat. He began his journey back; before he left the first mountain, his antlers loosened and fell off.

He had learned so much more about the forest during his second, longer stay there as a buck. He still wanted nothing more than to be a boy of the People, and he didn't want to shapeshift to buck any more than necessary, but he had to admit that the forest had begun to feel like his true home. He'd learned its many kinds paths, and how they followed the waterways and watered lands. His deepening knowledge of the forest scents lodged more firmly in his mind and heart. Scents of plant, animal, earth and water continually informed him and guided his every step, his every thought. And in the forest, he could be at his ease whether he was a boy or a buck. But in the knat, it was only as a boy that he could fit in.

He proceeded more carefully when he got into the lower lands. He gave himself a respite from constantly scanning for the scent of hunters, by going through one of the sinkhole areas. Besides their strange cool breezes and odd mists, sometimes the land was unstable; with so many better places to hunt, hunters avoided them.

* * *

When Tek reached the knat it was early morning, not long after dawn. He stayed in his buck shape and deliberately placed himself upwind, waiting for the entranceway to be unlashed for the day.

Several knaters came out and ranged themselves around the knat's walls as guards, with two of them at the entranceway.

Other than these guards, Woq was one of the early ones out, as Tek had expected: shapeshifters with a keen sense of smell longed for the fresher scents found outside of a knat.

Woq headed for the river but slowed to a stop when he caught Tek's scent. Unobtrusively he changed direction and went to where Tek was hiding in the brush.

Woq was grumpy. "You'd better watch out. I'm not all that full and you're looking meatier."

Tek shapeshifted to boy and got right to the point. "I know where your sister's bones are," he told Woq.

* * *

86

Woq insisted that Tek show him right away, so Tek led him to the sinkhole area. It was a long way from the knat; most of the way they travelled as buck and wolf. Tek always took care to keep a fair distance from Woq. His buck instinct told him that he could never completely trust him.

When Tek reached a particular sinkhole he stopped, turned into a boy and waited for Woq to get there. Woq slowed as he arrived, hackles raised and sniffing long and deliberately.

Woq turned into a young man and told Tek, "I don't smell anything."

"You won't, not until there's more warmth to move the air. We'll just have to wait."

While they waited, Woq shapeshifted to wolf to catch himself a fat squirrel or hare, while Tek browsed.

They both came back to the sinkhole after a few hours, and waited as buck and wolf; their sense of smell was keenest when they were animals. Finally Tek turned into a boy and said, "There. Smell that?"

Woq as wolf moved closer to the sinkhole to catch the wafts of cool air, and sniffed for a very long time.

Back as a young man Woq told Tek, "I couldn't smell anything."

Tek was surprised. "It smells of you — I mean it has to be your sister, and it smells of bone, damp bone. And . . . a few other things. Just traces though. Try again."

Woq did try again. He took his time, but in the end he shook his head. "Maybe. Possibly. But I can't be sure whether it's real or something that I . . . want to believe. I want it so much, to know she's finally been found. Deer can scent better than wolves . . . tell me more about it."

Tek explained that he'd been passing through the area when he caught a whiff that made him think that Woq might be somewhere around there, only still very far off. He concentrated on the scent and realized it wasn't Woq. It was similar but it was female, and it had many strange overlays, one of which was that it was no longer living. He followed the scent back to this hole.

"Let's go to another sinkhole that doesn't have this scent, or any other strong animal scent," Tek suggested. "Then we'll come back to this one and see if you can scent the difference."

When they returned to the sinkhole Woq as wolf crept closer to the hole than before, so close that he had to brace all four legs to keep from sliding down into it. He stretched his neck forward, closed his eyes and took a long time to absorb everything.

He backed slowly away from the hole, and shifted back into a young man. He was quieter and more subdued than Tek had ever seen him. "There *is* a difference," he said. "It's not so much of bone that I can smell, it's more of rotted skin, or hair or . . . yes. I could just barely smell it but it is really there. I'm not imagining it. So . . . this is where . . . where she is."

Woq looked up and around at the trees and the brush. "We were both terrified of the sinkhole lands when we were little," he said. "Woqri would never, ever have come to a place like this on her own."

"She could have fallen in, if she'd gotten lost and it was dark," Tek said, but Woq shook his head. "Never. She was too smart to travel when she couldn't see where she was going. And she was tough: if she got lost and it was getting dark, she would just climb a tree and stay in it until light."

Tek followed as Woq walked up the land that sloped down to the hole. "It would have been easy for Okat to drag or push her down this slope to the hole, after she'd killed her," Woq commented, with a tremor in his voice.

At the top of the slope the land was level for as far as they could see. It lay in a great solid swath with none of the odd hummocks and drops that marked a sinkhole area.

"So easy," Woq whispered hoarsely. "Okat led her here another way. Woqri wouldn't have realized that they were anywhere close to the sinkholes."

"Somewhere up here, close to here," Woq continued, "is where Okat killed Woqri."

Woq spoke with conviction, but Tek wondered that he could be sure, and he himself was not certain. Perhaps it had been an accident. Perhaps they'd been arguing, fighting, and Woqri fell down the slope and into the sinkhole.

"Let's see if we can find something up here," Tek suggested.

Woq seemed distracted, lost in thought, but he nodded.

As buck and wolf they scoured the area. It was an odd sight, if anyone had been watching, to see a buck and a wolf so close to each other with their noses right at the ground, now and then using hoof or paw to scrape aside the thick leaf litter under the trees and brush.

Tek's keener sense of smell found it, buried just under the surface of the soil. It was a slightly curved oak branch about the length and size of a man's forearm, with a heavy knot at one end. The other end had been honed to allow for a firm grip. It was a cudgel.

Some of it was damp with rot, but much of the hard dense wood was intact. Tek had found it because the scent of oak was out of place here. There were no oak trees anywhere nearby.

Tek snorted, getting Woq's attention. Woq sniffed when he came over, and then shapeshifted. With his fingers he swiped clots of soil away from the piece of oak, lifted it carefully from its earthen bed, and turned it over. Tek as buck took a sniff at the underside, stepped back and shapeshifted. "Blood," he said, "Your sister's blood." He didn't say more, but there were other scents as well. Skin. Bone. Brain.

Woq laid the piece of oak on the ground, shifted to wolf and sniffed for himself. Shifting back, "Yes," he said. "Driven deep into the crevices of the knot."

Lifting the oak piece Woq gripped it and gave it a downward shake, assessing its weight and balance. "Easy," he said softly, but his voice cracked. "So easy to club Woqri when she'd looked away. So ea—"

Woq's voice broke into hoarse wracking sobs. Tek quickly and cautiously backed away. He was worried about what Woq might do next.

Inconsolable grief changed rapidly to a terrible, consuming anger. Woq shapeshifted to wolf in a blinding rage. He wanted to kill — anyone, anything. He sprang at Tek.

Tek shifted to buck and ran, prepared to go into the highlands if necessary. But he was still in the lowlands and hills, where there was the real danger of coming across hunters from one of the knats. He ran into the wind, doing his best to avoid the areas that he knew hunters preferred.

Even so the chase might have been a long and dangerous one, if Tek hadn't caught the scent of marmot out ahead of him. He led Woq right to it, jumping over it and bounding well beyond it.

The marmot put up a fight but Woq was an unstoppable killer that morning.

Tek waited and then circled back downwind of Woq. Woq in his wolf shape was still eating the marmot — slowly, unenthusiastically. Woq eventually noticed Tek watching him. Morosely he continued to chew until he had finished the fleshier parts. Then he shifted back into a young man.

"I lost . . . myself," Woq told Tek, which was the closest he would come to apologizing. "Wasn't really hungry enough for that marmot, but it . . . helped, I guess.

"You go on ahead of me, Tek, back to the knat. I'm going back to the . . . to where she died, to get that cudgel — but wait. You've been away. There are some things I should tell you first."

Woq told Tek that while he'd been gone S'Och's oldest daughter Ochri had been chosen to replace S'Och as clan mother. So far Okat was acting very quiet about it, but no one really believed that she had changed for the better. "She just knows she can't get away with as much," Woq said, "now that S'Och is not there for her to hide behind."

Woq also told Tek that many of the men had left a few days ago to raid some knats further upriver. That was the reason for the guards. No one was expecting an attack because the knat was so large and had such a stout wall. But at this time of year, it was a precaution while so many of the men were gone. "Guard duty is very boring. You'll have to do it too," Woq told Tek.

From Woq Tek also learned the story that had been circulated by S'Kaw's clanhouse to explain his absence. Supposedly, he had gone back to his birth knat for a visit. "So approach the knat from that direction," Woq told Tek. "Not that anyone will be paying any attention to you."

90

Chapter 12

The Frost Moon[2] began with much colder weather, and one night there was a light snow. The knat's women and girls were still busy with the last harvesting and gleanings, and with preparing the foods for winter storage. Bear pelts that hadn't already been made supple were softened; deer hides that had not yet been readied for clothing were scraped, softened and smoked. Boys fished, hunted and brought in fire wood. Men who hadn't gone on the raid hunted, and patched the bark of the clanhouses for the winter.

After being gone for nearly a month the men returned from their raiding at the middle of the Frost Moon, begrimed but jubilant. It had been a great success. Substantial wrongs had been righted; prowess proven; warrior skills honed. And the filchings had been good. Among the more substantial takings were two canoes and some valuable stores.

Injuries were inevitable. None were severe, but that didn't stop Ani from having hysterics when she first saw that Roh had bloody wrappings on his bow arm.

Roh had been exemplary during the raiding. Gone was the old lazy Roh who would have hung well back from the more intense fighting. Even so, his arm had not been wounded in any pitched battle. On impulse he had grabbed an especially large, fine bear skin from a clanhouse. He wanted it for Ani, and for their child when it was born near the end of the Cold Moon.[3] The bulky pelt slowed his flight, and a lucky shot by a pursuing knater sent an arrow through the flesh of his upper arm. He hung on to the pelt though and proudly presented it to Ani after he'd convinced her that his wound

---

[2] November, usually.
[3] December, usually.

was not really all that serious. He had used the ointments they carried in their pouches, to keep his wound from festering.

* * *

Not long after the men returned from the raiding, a brief period of warmer weather came. The knat redoubled its preparations for the winter, finishing the harvesting, the gathering and the messy outside tasks that would otherwise have to be left until spring.

It was on one of those fine weather days that the shaman, Woq and Woq's older brother, who knew Woq's shapeshifting secret, journeyed to where Woqri had been killed. They did not tell anyone where they were going, or why.

On the land above the slope down to the sinkhole, they lit a small fire and the shaman led a special mourning ceremony for Woqri.

Most of the shaman's words were prayers, but there was a part where he was to speak as specifically as possible about Woqri and how she had died. Then he was supposed to combine that with an exhortation to the deceased's spirit to be at peace. He had given much thought to what he would say, but when it came time to actually speak of Woqri and her death the words he had chosen seemed hollow and inadequate to him. Perhaps it was because this ceremony was being performed in the forest, far from the knat, and so long after the child Woqri had died. Perhaps it was because of the glowering faces of Woq and his brother as they, listening to his words, kept their angry gazes fixed on the fire. Or perhaps it was his own abhorrence for the wrongness of this death, that he was unable to quell at this time, in this place. His words guttered out. He tried again, but his second try failed too.

He began again with new words, speaking simply and truly of an evil in the young Okat's breast that had cost Woqri her life. Then he tried to bind these words to the exhortation, but he could not think of a way to do it. He could not think of a way to twine a cold–hearted murder with peace for the dead girl's spirit.

Cold damp air rushed up the slope from the sinkhole. Bats followed and flew in a circle above the three mourners. It happened so quickly that the shaman and Woq's brother simply stared at the bats in wonder. But Woq yelled, "Woqri! Woqri!" and shifted to wolf. As wolf he watched the encircling bats intently, woofing at them, while he backed slowly away from the fire.

To the shaman it looked as if Woq might be trying to draw something away from the bats, something that he alone could see. The shaman wasn't sure what he himself should do, if anything. He had some herbs in his bag; some semah[4] for summoning the spirits, and weengush[5] for soothing them. He took both out and held them up, waving them so that Woq could see and smell them. He would trust Woq's decision, whether to put either one or both of them into the fire.

But the bats suddenly closed on the semah, tearing at it and biting the shaman's hand. The shaman shook them off, and the semah fell into the fire.

The fire flared blue, and Woq rushed toward it, whining and growling. Then the blue flare was gone, and the bats flew away.

Woq shifted back into a young man. He was shaking and his eyes were very wide. "Some part of Woqri's spirit is here," he told the shaman and his brother. "But it's not very strong."

"Perhaps it will now be able to take its journey west," the shaman replied.

That was not what Woq wanted, though he did not say so to the shaman.

He thought he had seen a vague, wavery wolf–like spirit floating among the circling bats. He had tried to draw it toward him, away from the bats. He wanted the wolf spirit, which he thought might be Woqri's, to join with him to defeat their enemy Okat. But after it rose above the bats and veered toward him, it dissipated.

He did not tell the shaman any of this. "Yes, perhaps," he said. "Perhaps it will journey west. But maybe it can't go away, until its death has been avenged."

* * *

Woqri's weak, faded spirit watched the three mourners leave. Her spirit had recognized the shaman but she was not certain of the two

---

[4] tobacco
[5] sweetgrass

men with him. They looked familiar, like some of the members of her family. But she did not know who they were.

It was the younger one that had done something very strange — something that she had not known that any of the People could do. He had turned himself into a wolf. Stranger still, while he was in the wolf form he had clearly beckoned to her.

She had resided among the bats for so long; she did not want to leave them. But as she watched the wolf, she was reminded strongly of her brother Woq. She wondered about him for the first time in a long while. Semah smoke rose from the fire below her and eased her away from the bats and further above the fire in the updraft. She tried to float closer to the wolf but her essence dissipated with the semah smoke. Then the bats left and she could not follow them back into the cave.

After the mourners left Woqri tried to gather herself back together. Even at full strength she was weak and light. She could barely turn over a leaf, and then only with great effort. She could do almost nothing but float and observe what was around her. The slightest breeze shifted her sideways. She was aware of forest sounds, but they were muted as if distant.

Her spirit was alone in this place. The last she remembered was that Okat had brought her here, to harvest some exceptionally fine spruce resin. The spirit wondered where Okat was, and where the special spruce tree was. Okat had told her that they were almost there. They had stopped at a pine sapling to make a basket from strips of its bark. She was excited; she was looking forward to the taste of the resin as it softened into a gum in her mouth. She was kneeling, starting to weave the bark strips, when her recollection as a person ended. Her next recollection was as a spirit in the cave below the sinkhole.

She did not know that many years had passed. She thought it was still the time when she had been the young girl Woqri, and her brother Woq was a young boy.

* * *

Much later that day a lone wolf came to the place. It looked all around until it saw the faint, wavery spirit of Woqri. The wolf came up to the spirit and then shape shifted into a young man — the same young man who had been one of the mourners.

"Woqri," this young man said, "I am Woq. I am your brother Woq." He immediately turned back into a wolf, to watch the spirit's reaction to his words.

Woqri's spirit was barely able to hear what the young man said, but she thought he said her brother's name. The spirit floated very close to the wolf, looking at it questioningly. Woq could not see his sister's spirit very well, but from what he could see he surmised that she was having difficulty understanding him.

Painstakingly, Woq and his sister's spirit worked out a way to communicate. Woq spoke very slowly and simply, repeating over and over again what he wanted the spirit to know, guessing at the questions she would have, and asking her about things he wanted to know. Woqri's spirit concentrated herself until she was able to turn a sheltered leaf one way for 'yes', and the other way for 'no'. If she simply fluttered the leaf, it meant she did not know.

As the day ended, Woq asked Woqri to return to the knat, and Woqri agreed to try. If she succeeded, she was to come to where he slept in the clanhouse, and turn over an oak leaf that he would leave lying on a small shelf beside his sleeping space. He explained that he might be away on a hunt, but would always check on the leaf when he got back.

* * *

The Cold Moon[6] began, when the power of life in the land and rivers slept, and the frost spirits with their lipless mouths and jagged teeth came out to cavort in the darkness. The hunters were gone longer, having to go further away to find prey.

The day of least light, when the Sky World's fire burnt lowest, was still about three long notches[7] away.

The Ochri clanhouse was as ready for winter as the others. Everything was going along smoothly. Ochri had proven her worthiness to be the new clan mother. She was strong–minded, diligent and fair. Nearly everyone in the clanhouse cooperated with

---

[6] December, usually.

[7] three weeks

95

her. There was general approval for the way she disposed of the disagreements that arose.

For her part Ochri felt herself come fully and naturally into her new clan mother role. She had many good plans to enhance the strengths the clanhouse, and ease its burdens.

The one challenge that she knew she still had to face, was a major confrontation with Okat. Okat had been unusually quiet and cooperative since the tenth–day ceremony for their mother. But Ochri was not lulled by Okat's seeming compliance with the clanhouse ways. She was certain that Okat had not changed for the better. Long and discriminating observation had taught her that there was nothing inside Okat for any goodness to build upon. This was confirmed by a sour, hideous expression on Okat's face that Ochri sometimes saw, when Okat thought that she was not being observed.

Ochri had the wisdom and knowledge to anticipate, sooner or later, a challenge to her authority by Okat. But even so, she underestimated Okat. She did not realize that Okat's quietness masked a new, deeper well of evil, growing inside her. She attributed Okat's silence and bad humor to nothing more than her sullen realization that without S'Och there to protect her, her openly vicious ways would no longer be tolerated.

Early on a chill afternoon, Ochri and one of the daughters of her clanhouse went to a forest bog to gather some medicinal fungi. The girl was Oji. She was fifteen, the child of one of Ochri's cousins.

Ochri had been making the trip annually for many years, from the time she was Oji's age. Now that she was clan mother, this was the last time she would go to gather the fungi. In the future Oji would do it.

It was well known in the clanhouse that Ochri and the girl were going on the trip; it had been postponed several times because Ochri had been so busy.

A cold rain was threatening, or perhaps a wet snow, but they went ahead, taking only their short knives and some baskets. It would not be a long trip since the bog was not far away, and danger was unlikely. It was not yet the time of year when a wild animal might be desperate enough to hunt close to the knat.

When they were nearly to the bog Ochri got strong feeling of peril. But it was indefinite, other than that it seemed to her that the forest had become much too quiet.

Suddenly three deer burst from the brush ahead of them and ran past them. Something upwind of the deer had startled them.

Ochri reacted quickly; she and Oji put their baskets down, drew their knives and, quickly and silently, turned back.

They soon reached a travelled path that went alongside a stream. In a gusty downpour, Ochri directed the girl to climb with her up into a large spruce there. They had not been up in the spruce's dense, heavy boughs very long when a panther stalked by, from the direction of the bog.

Ochri had a better view of the panther than Oji. As she watched the panther, it turned into her sister Okat for a few moments, and then into a small black bear. The bear cast on either side of the path for scent, but the pelting rain had washed scent out, even for a bear's more sensitive nose. The bear then continued on the path toward the knat, travelling quickly. It seemed to Ochri that it was following the path, rather than scent.

When the bear was well away, Oji spoke to Ochri quietly.

"Auntie, I think I saw that panther turn into a bear. Is that . . . possible?" The girl had not been able to see Okat in those moments between panther and bear; or if she had, she was in too much doubt to speak of it.

Ochri whispered that she was not certain, and that when they got back to the knat she would have to consult with the shaman about it.

In the tree, sheltered from the heavy rain by the spruce's dense canopy, Ochri thought through what had just happened.

She did not question what she had seen.

Not long after she became clan mother, the shaman visited her, and spoke to her in private about the old shapeshifter stories. She had been rather busy at the time, with one of the first crises she faced as the new clan mother. She could barely repress her impatience as he droned through several of the stories; she thought he was just using them, in a clumsy way, to warn her of how a person in power, such as herself, must search out the true nature of everyone around her, and must watch others for changes to the worst. She realized that his visit was an honor, but she felt she already knew what he was warning her about.

She had thanked him politely for coming to see her, but she had not really understood him.

She understood him now. He had been trying to tell her that her sister Okat was a dangerous shapeshifter.

She now realized — the panther that had disrupted her mother's mourning ceremony — that had been her sister Okat. Ochri remembered the wild rage in the panther's scream, and that the panther had been coming in her direction before the hunters blocked its way. And she remembered the terrible power in its leap at one of the hunters. It would have killed him, if it hadn't been for the other wild animals in the knat that bizarre night. She spared a moment to wonder . . . were they shapeshifters too?

Ochri pondered why her sister Okat would be waiting for her at the bog, and concluded that Okat was intent upon killing her, making it look like she had been attacked and killed by a wild panther. Panthers were not very common in the area, but they were the one animal that would kill even when not in need of food.

Ochri saw that she had been completely mistaken about Okat's surly quietness since their mother's tenth–day ceremony. Okat, having lost their mother's powerful protection, had *not* accepted her demoted position. Instead, she had become a much more dangerous evil than ever before, because she had become stealthy.

Cruel, vicious Okat, with a bear or panther's sense of smell, and the power of muscle, tooth and claw . . . Ochri understood that she was in mortal danger, and nearly defenseless. Even this tree, which would protect them from an ordinary bear or panther, would not protect them from her shapeshifting sister Okat.

Muscle, tooth and claw . . . an innate terror nearly froze Ochri's blood, but she forced her fear back, and resolved to give the unequal battle her best fight.

Okat would come back, after she reached the knat and saw that they had not yet returned.

The rainstorm had gone in the direction of the knat; the rain was already slackening where they were. If they did not leave soon, Okat would find them in the tree by scent.

As did most of the women of the People, Ochri knew a lot about animals' sense of smell from listening to the men's hunting talk. As Ochri and Oji climbed out of the tree, Ochri tried to choose, based on the wind's direction, the best way to hide their scent from Okat while they returned to the knat. She determined that their best chance was to make a long loop around the direct path, by going far to the south.

Ochri and Oji set out rapidly and silently, with their short knives at the ready. They stopped only for each of them to pick up a fallen branch, stout enough to use as a weapon. Oji obeyed Ochri without delay or questions. She understood that her auntie felt endangered and was urgently trying to get them back to the knat safely. She willingly put her trust in the older, admired woman.

Ochri's ruse might have worked if Okat had gone all the way to the knat before turning back. But Okat guessed that she had missed them, and turned back much sooner. She reached the spruce tree not long after Ochri and the girl had left, and easily followed their scent south. When she realized why they had headed south, she cut across the arc they were making to waylay them before they reached the knat.

Ochri did not see the panther — her shapeshifting sister Okat — until moments before it sprang. In those few moments she knew that her life was nearly over, but she had decided that she would not go weakly, or with fear–glazed eyes. She shouted to Oji to run for her life and she faced the panther with her stick raised in both hands, and her knife secure against the palm of one hand.

The stick deflected the attack just enough for Ochri to jab once at the panther with her knife, but it barely grazed the panther's shoulder as they both went down. The panther easily twisted and seized Ochri's neck in its jaws while tearing at her chest and belly with its claws. Ochri struggled but she was pinned helplessly below the panther on the ground.

Okat wanted her sister to die slowly, primarily from the evisceration of her belly. Her teeth in her sister's neck, and her front claws ripping at her sister's arms and chest, were to hold her down, and to weaken and disable her. She gave little thought to the girl Oji. There would be plenty of time after she killed her sister, to chase down the fleeing girl.

She was so intent on prolonging her sister's death, that she was completely surprised by a heavy blow on her panther skull.

Oji had not run away, as Ochri had told her to do.

While Oji was hiding in the tree with her aunt, she had in fact seen Okat in the shapeshift between panther and bear. And when Okat as panther attacked Ochri, Oji was certain that Okat would chase her down to kill her too. She chose to fight back, to fight against this abrupt termination of her life by the evil Okat. If she had to die this day, she would die just as bravely as her beloved auntie Ochri.

Oji smote the panther on its head, between its eyes, shattering her heavy stick. Then with a furious snarl she charged the panther with her short knife.

Momentarily stunned by the blow, Okat still reacted quickly. She gave her sister's neck a vicious jerk, abruptly ending her life, and in the next instant she sprang to meet the girl's charge.

Oji, using momentum and a desperate jab, got her knife into one of Okat's eyes, lacerating it and cutting deeply into the eye socket, before she was overpowered.

Okat killed the girl, despite the pain exploding in her left eye.

The pain in her eye and its blindness were terrible for Okat, but that was not the worst of it. The worst was the gross disfigurement of her beautiful face, because it meant that she would never be able to return to the knat of her birth, as one of the People. Everyone would see her lacerated eye, and there was no explanation she could give for it, that would be believed.

Her birthright — her existence in her clanhouse as one of the People — had been destroyed in an instant by the girl's knife. In that one instant Okat went from being a powerful shapeshifting woman, to a deformed outcast. Over Oji's body, she shrieked her fury and rage.

Chapter 13

Woq was away hunting, but Tek, S'Kaw and Tsihi heard the distant panther screams, with their keen hearing. S'Kaw and Tsihi began asking among the clanhouses, to determine whether everyone could be accounted for as safe.

It wasn't long before concern for Ochri and Oji raced through the knat. When it was clear that they had not returned from the bog, a group from several of the clanhouses formed to go look for them. Tsihi was keen to go, but S'Kaw would not allow her, with a child in her womb, to leave the knat. S'Kaw and Tek were part of the group, though, along with some others from their clanhouse.

When the group reached the area by the spruce tree, even in their human form, S'Kaw and Tek picked up the scent of Ochri, Oji and Okat, heading south. As the rest of the group continued toward the bog, S'Kaw told one of the boys of her clanhouse that she and Tek were going to leave the group to follow some markings they had found. Then as they went south following the scent, they marked their way with broken branches and hastily blazed bark on saplings.

This was the first time that Tek had gone anywhere alone with S'Kaw. He had avoided the stern, distant clan mother, and she had deliberately kept him at a distance. Now they worked quickly in a solemn, grim silence, marking the way together.

The rest of the group continued toward the bog, finding the empty baskets on the way there. When they did not find Ochri or the girl at the bog, they went back to where they found the baskets and fanned out, though still within hearing distance of each other. When that yielded nothing, the boy told them that S'Kaw and Tek were following some markings further back. The group went back with him and then to the south, following the trail markings left by S'Kaw and Tek.

They were searching in the fading light when they heard S'Kaw's shouts ahead of them. S'Kaw came toward them out of the dusk, telling them that she and Tek had found the bodies of Ochri and Oji.

Tek had followed Okat's scent when it split from Ochri's and the girl's; S'Kaw had continued to follow Ochri's and the girl's. Because Okat had taken a shorter route, Tek reached the place where Ochri and Oji died before S'Kaw.

Both victims were horribly mauled: it was clear to Tek that Okat had spent a considerable amount of her fury on them. But Tek also saw their knives and the shattered staff. It was plain that they had put up a fight.

In the time before S'Kaw arrived, Tek shapeshifted to buck. He was then able to easily smell Okat's fresh blood, and from that he knew she had been wounded in some way. He also determined that she had left the area going further south. And in the gloaming, he saw the spirits of Ochri and the girl. They were nearby, intent on helping each other, smoothing each other's shredded clothing and hair. When Tek approached them they turned to look at him. The girl seemed uninterested in Tek, but the eyes of Ochri's spirit narrowed and looked back at Tek intently.

The two spirits then left, going in the direction of the knat. It was as if some unseen compulsion made them go to where they had spent so much of their lives.

S'Kaw arrived and conferred with Tek. She sent him to the knat to tell the shaman what had happened. She also warned him to be careful, in case Okat returned and was not yet satiated. But on the way to the knat Tek did not come across Okat's scent; nor did he see or hear anything more of her.

The shaman listened to the terrible news gravely. Most of the knat would think that Ochri and Oji had been killed by a wild panther, but he and the shapeshifters knew, or would know, that Okat had killed them.

He sent someone to tell the clanhouses of the news of Ochri and Oji's deaths, and to help them organize to retrieve the bodies.

Later when everyone had returned and the knat's entranceway had been lashed closed for the night, Okat's family noticed that Okat was nowhere in the clanhouse, or the knat.

During the night, S'Kaw waited as hawk, perched above the main entrance of her clanhouse. She was waiting for the visitation that a deceased clan mother's spirit made to the other clanhouses, on the night of her death, or on the following night. The clan mother spirit came to each clanhouse and stood before it, before continuing to the next.

When Ochri's spirit came in her clan mother robes and stood before the S'Kaw clanhouse, she was accompanied by the girl Oji's spirit. S'Kaw as hawk flew down to the ground to meet them. Ochri's spirit was taken aback by the large hawk's presence, but she then recognized that the hawk and clan mother S'Kaw were one and the same. Ochri's spirit knelt to sit with the hawk and commune with it.

S'Kaw shapeshifted into a woman. As a woman she could no longer see the two spirits but she whispered to them, asking them to show her where Okat had been wounded. When S'Kaw shapeshifted back into a hawk, she was able to see Oji's spirit make a knife–stab gesture, and then cover her left eye.

The next morning a brief search was made for Okat by some of her family, in the environs of the knat, but she was not found.

*　*　*

On the third day of the mourning for Ochri and the girl, one of the hunting parties returned with kill — two deer and a bear. Their joy in bringing such bounty was cut short when they learned of the tragedy that had occurred during their absence. Some of the younger ones wanted to go right back out to hunt for the panther, in case it was still in the vicinity. But they were prevailed upon to at least wait until the mourning period was over.

Woq had been in the returning hunting party. When he reached his clanhouse he was told that the shaman wanted to meet with him. He went first to put away his weapons; in his small sleeping compartment he glanced at the oak leaf he had left for Woqri's spirit.

It was turned over.

Quietly Woq closed himself into his compartment and shapeshifted into a wolf. As a wolf he saw that Woqri's spirit was there, watching him. Her spirit was clearer to him now and more like a girl than wolf. As he watched the spirit approached him. When it waved its translucent hands in front of his face, he felt the air stir there.

Woq changed back into a young man and whispered, "Try that again, Woqri." And again, he felt the air stir in front of his face. Woqri's spirit had been consolidating her small presence.

Woq went to visit the shaman. When he arrived, the shaman sent one of his daughters to summon S'Kaw. He also asked his family for privacy. The nearby living compartments emptied, and his family stayed at a distance. Some of them sat by a fire, singing a low song, fitting for a mourning time.

Woq felt the same stir of air in his face; in this way he understood that his sister Woqri's spirit had travelled to the shaman's with him. He told the shaman of this. He then took a small feather, and after putting it on the mat, he asked Woqri's spirit to turn it over. In the still air of the shaman's compartment, the feather turned over.

"So," the shaman observed drily, "it seems that at least one of our shapeshifters can communicate with the spirits of our dead."

"Sometimes, with some of them, it is possible," Woq responded with reserve.

When S'Kaw arrived, the shaman told them, "Most of the knat believe that Ochri and the girl died because the mourning for S'Och was flawed. They believe that the additional ceremonies held afterward did not repair the damage. They think that S'Och's spirit sent a panther to kill them, to placate her angry spirit.

"We know the truth. Okat killed them, but she did not get away unscathed. Her left eye was cut . . . it would be an ugly wound, and the eye is probably blind. We do not think that she will return openly as a person of the knat. Her vanity will stop her, besides not being able to explain how she came to be maimed.

"We also know for certain now, that long ago Okat killed the girl Woqri. Then at S'Och's tenth–day ceremony she would have killed again if the other shapeshifters, and the power in the rattle, had not stopped her.

"I do not think it will stop here. She will kill again, and again. And you shapeshifters will be among her first victims. Your keen senses can detect her when others cannot, and you have the natural weaponry of your animal shapes, though it is not as great as hers.

"Anyone that Okat has a grudge against — like Ani and Roh, or anyone who knows her secret — like you, and me — are not safe from her either. No one —"

"We must go after her," interrupted Woq. "We must hunt her. Surely you both can see that? And I have a plan. We will confide in some of our best hunters, to this extent: we will tell them that Okat and I are both shapeshifters, and then I will show them that it is so by shapeshifting before them. Then we will explain all the killings that Okat has done. Yes? Because when they know all this, they will understand that she must be hunted down. And I will go with them on the hunt. I will find her scent and together we will hunt and hunt until we have found her and destroyed her. It has to be — it is the only way to protect ourselves and the rest of the knat."

S'Kaw disagreed. "You come here fresh from a hunt, Woq, and the shock from the news of these deaths is still very fresh. Naturally you want to act immediately. Decisively.

"But there are many ways for your plan to go wrong. And the worst of it is this: in the forest Okat will always out hunt you. Always." S'Kaw gazed at Woq and pounded her fist into the palm of her other hand. The dry splat punctuated her certainty. "Recollect, Woq, that as a bear she can scent better than any of us, even Tek. And as a panther she can easily hunt at night. She knows *all* of our hunter ways. Hunt her down in the forest? No. In the forest you will all die by her tooth and claw — you first of all, Woq.

"Our strength lies here in this knat. Here we must watch and wait. We must see what she does — if she does anything. If she attacks our hunting parties in the forest, then in desperation, we may have to use your plan, Woq. But if she attacks any of us in the knat, then we will have a better chance against her, if we are watchful, and can work together against her."

Woq did not like S'Kaw's advice, but he reluctantly accepted the wisdom of her words.

The shaman said, "She can enter the knat secretly as a shapeshifter. We know that one of her shapes is either winged, or is small enough to get through the knat wall.

"Woq, the other shapeshifters have been checking along the wall at night, for a scent of Okat in her small, unknown shape. So far though, it has not been found."

Their talk turned to maintaining a watch over the knat at night, and to signals to alert each other if Okat ever came back.

Woq knew that his sister's spirit had accompanied him to the meeting, but he did not know that Ochri's spirit had come too.

Ochri's spirit had mightily resisted the great pull to begin her journey. If Woq had been in his wolf shape he would have seen her spirit was there. He would have seen the reaction of Ochri's spirit when the shaman said that Okat had murdered Woqri.

Afterward, Ochri's spirit followed Woqri's spirit , and obtained the truth from it about Woqri's death.

* * *

The four shapeshifters divided themselves into two pairs to keep watch at night. S'Kaw and Tsihi took the first halves of the nights: as birds they were much less conspicuous in case someone in the knat was up and about. Tek and Woq took the quieter second halves of the nights.

Woqri's spirit accompanied them sometimes, or they saw her wandering through the knat. They also saw Ochri's spirit there until her tenth–day ceremony, but not afterward.

On the day after the tenth–day ceremony, a group of younger hunters did go out in search of the panther. Most of them were from the Ochri clanhouse. Woq went too, but he found no fresh scent of Okat where the rest of the hunters were willing to go. They did not find the panther, though they did slay a deer, which gave them some yield for their effort.

* * *

Over the rest of the Cold Moon the shaman visited the clanhouses during in the evenings and, for the first time in many years, it was the old stories of shapeshifters that he told to the people gathered around their fires. He told the stories with such verve and passion that the knaters' imaginings became greatly stirred by them. Some, remembering the strangeness of the five wild animals that had been in the knat on the night of S'Och's tenth day ceremony, wondered aloud whether any of those animals could have been shapeshifters. The buck, in particular, had made that strange low bow, so unlike what an ordinary buck would do . . .

106

Tek listened to the shaman's shapeshifter stories with mixed feelings. He understood that the shaman was preparing the people of the knat, in case any of the shapeshifters had to be revealed to them. But Tek felt an exposure because his animal shape — a buck — primarily meant food and hides to the knaters. They would readily identify with a wolf, a hawk or an owl. But not with a buck.

Soon Tek had other worries.

His dreams took odd, frightening turns again — like his dreams before the first time he shapeshifted into a buck. As before, most of these dreams began with Tek hunting, except that now he was not hunting deer. Instead, he was hunting small game — hare, raccoon, squirrel, even skunk, with his fingers flexing eagerly on his short bow, his arrow cocked to let fly.

In the earlier deer hunting dreams, this was when Tek felt himself changing into a buck — right before another hunter loosed an arrow aimed at his buck heart. In the new dreams, when Tek felt himself changing he immediately reacted in an explosive rush, from dream knowledge that a predator was springing — though the type of predator was never very clear.

If it was hare he'd been hunting, then the hare in his dream bounded and weaved desperately. If it was raccoon or squirrel then it raced madly for a tree to climb. If a skunk, then it flipped and sprayed, but that dream was the worst of all because just before he woke up from it he had the realization that the spray would not stop the predator.

Tek supposed he should go to the shaman and tell him about the new dreams, or go to the forest to encourage the release of the new shape. But he put off both, dreading the actual knowledge of which prey animal his new shape was going to be. He told himself that the dreams were not very insistent yet. He hoped that if he waited . . . maybe the shape might change to something . . . better. At least, until he knew for sure, he could hope for that.

Tek stopped hunting small game altogether when the new dreams began. He fished instead, chipping holes through the river ice to drop in his stone–weighted bone hooks.

He had not eaten deer meat since he had first shapeshifted into a buck. Now he did not want to eat the meat of small game either.

He tried to hide it, but both S'Kaw and Tsihi noticed, and one evening S'Kaw drew him aside and asked him bluntly if he was having new dreams. He reluctantly admitted to her that he was having dreams of turning into several different small game animals.

"Odd," S'Kaw responded. "Odd for there to be more than one animal at a time. Unless . . ."

She dismissed her unspoken thought and brusquely told Tek not to fight these dreams. "Get to the forest as soon as the dreams strengthen," she told him. She also told him to make himself eat the small game meat, at least until he knew for sure which animal he was going to be. He was still too thin, she said. The meat would give him strength that he needed. "And let Woq know about this," she ordered. "But not the shaman — not yet. I'll tell Tsihi. Don't you bother her with it."

Tsihi's belly was enlarging with the baby growing in her womb, and S'Kaw was increasingly protective of her granddaughter's wellbeing. Tsihi still did most of her usual duties but S'Kaw forbade her to do some of them. She also kept everyone who was ill away from Tsihi, and she ordered everyone to bring their fretful matters to her rather than to Tsihi.

Tek knew that S'Kaw and Tsihi had argued about whether Tsihi would be allowed to do a share of the nightly watches for Okat. Most of the time Tsihi deferred to her grandmother's wishes, but in this she insisted on being allowed to do her part. She argued that the shared burden was much lighter with her contribution. S'Kaw grudgingly allowed it, but decreed that it must stop when the Sap Moon[8] began, when Tsihi would be only two moons away from birthing.

When Tek told Woq about the new dreams, Woq took the news quietly, but Tek knew he was disappointed. Woq so much wanted another wolf like himself. But Tek could not help what his shape was, and his buck shape had proved to have some uses after all. A buck's sense of smell was much better than Woq's as wolf. And the slashing hooves of a roused buck could at least do some damage.

---

[8] March, usually.

Chapter 14

On a night about halfway through the Cold Moon[9] there was a commotion in the clanhouse where Ani and Roh lived. Ani's contractions had begun. Early the next morning she went with some of the women to the childbirth hut, a short distance from the knat. She labored all that day and most of the night; near dawn a son was born of her.

The shaman arranged for the hut to be guarded throughout the birthing. That was unusual, except in times of war. But unexpected, violent death had so recently stalked not far from the knat. The knat heeded its shaman's precaution.

Woq was one of three guards watching over the hut when the child was born. Woqri's spirit was also there, as was Tsihi as owl, perched in a nearby tree. S'Kaw and Tek kept watch in the knat.

Not long after the child's first cries broke the silence of the night, Woqri's spirit and Tsihi as owl saw Ochri's lurching spirit approach the hut from the east, making frenzied, grotesque gestures of an attacking animal. The spirit seemed to be weak, laboring with great effort to move and to make the gestures. It approached from downwind of the hut and the knat: if Okat was coming from that direction her scent would not be detected at the hut. Woqri's spirit alerted Woq, and Tsihi flew silently in the direction that Ochri's spirit had come from. Soon she found Okat approaching as a panther and hooted the signal: Okat was near. Okat was coming.

Woqri's spirit and Woq had devised several ways for Woqri's spirit to communicate with Woq when he could not see her. When the spirit gave Woq the right direction to look for Okat, Woq told the two other guards that he was certain he heard noises coming

_____

[9] December, usually.

from that direction. As they readied themselves and strained to see movement in the darkness, there were shouts from the knat: Tek and S'Kaw had heard Tsihi's signal and were rousing the knat. Soon hunters would be spilling out of the knat and converging on the hut.

* * *

Okat had been back in the area for several days. The lacerated flesh around her wounded eye had scabbed over, though she would never see from that eye again.

She had come back to find out if Ani's child had been born yet. When she saw Ani, just outside the knat's wall, her belly huge with her unborn child, she settled down to wait.

During the wait she minimized her scent and kept well hidden in her chipmunk shape. She positioned herself so that the wind would favor her, carrying the scents of the knat and hut toward her, while carrying her own scent further away. It irritated her that Ochri's spirit was still around, and followed her everywhere, but she had no fear of it. It could not hurt her, or stop her from doing anything she wanted to do. And the strength of Ochri's spirit was clearly fading. It was torn between wanting to go on its journey west, and wanting to thwart her.

Only a few days after Okat arrived in the area, she caught the scent of Ani and other women coming to her in the breeze, from the birthing hut.

All that day and long into the night as she waited, she stoked her hatred for the stupid, ugly girl who had stolen her husband.

In the night she also caught the scent of Tsihi and the three hunters who were at the hut, including Woq's.

She had not planned to go after Woq and the other shapeshifters until after she had finished with Ani and Roh. But here was Woq, enticingly vulnerable . . . so foolishly overconfident.

She waffled, but then resolved to stick with her original plan after all. Each in their proper turn. Each at the proper time.

All of her planning dissolved though when she heard the newborn child's first cries. In that moment, pain pounded her wounded eye and blood lust propelled her. She darted from her hiding place, shifted to person and then to panther, and surged toward the hut, ready to kill any and everything in her path, and at the hut.

As she got closer she saw Ochri's spirit lurching toward the hut ahead of her; she heard Tsihi's unnatural hooting. Then before she got much closer, there was suddenly a lot of noise coming from the knat.

She wavered, and everything taken together chilled her fury. Hard–learned caution won out; her plan reasserted itself. She slowed, and then turned aside. But before she left she released a tremendous volley of savage panther screams.

In the hut Ani had been blissfully absorbing every detail of her beautiful little boy. She was awash in wonder. He was so very well formed; his first cries were so strong. He was absolutely perfect. She was caressing his cheek, cooing to him, when a panther screamed, very close by. Its harsh, sobbing voice reverberated through the hut. Ani convulsively hugged her son against her breast. Her joy evaporated. A great fear for her newborn son filled her heart.

The further Okat got from the hut and the knat, the better she felt. The throbbing in her blind eye subsided; her anger stilled and her thoughts cleared. Yes, she would wait now; she would wait for the right time and place to exact her perfect revenge on Ani and Roh. Then she would pick off the four shapeshifters one by one, and after them, the shaman. There would be still more. She would terrorize the knat. Perhaps over time she would eventually destroy it. By waiting for the right opportunities, by being patient and stealthy, she would be unstoppable.

*   *   *

In the morning Ani took her child to the river for its ritual bathing. Normally only the women of the mother and child's clanhouse accompanied them, but on this occasion most of the knat attended, including many armed men. The knat had been awakened early that morning by shouts that there was a panther near the birthing hut. Then the panther's wild screams tore at everyone's nerves and chilled their souls. At first light the hunters searched for the panther, but found only signs that it had left the area. There was a collective sigh of relief, and the knat looked upon the healthy newborn — its newest member — as a good omen. While Ani bathed it at the river's shore, thanking Sky Mother for the safe birth of her child, many knaters silently offered thanks to the Good Twin, that the night had not ended in another violent, untimely death. And they prayed that the panther, now representing a great evil in their minds, would go far away from them and never, ever return.

Woq had told two more of his close relatives about himself and the other shapeshifters, and also about Woqri's fate, and about her spirit being in the knat with them. Now three in his clanhouse knew the secrets: his older brother who had known before, an older sister and a younger brother. Woq told them because he wanted them to know what had happened to their sister, and because he had a presentiment that he was going to need their help if Okat ever did return to the knat.

Later that morning Woq stationed these three to keep the other knaters away from the area that was downwind of the birthing hut. Woq and Tek were there as wolf and buck, trying to discover the scent of Okat's third shape. In this they were aided by Woqri's spirit: it guided Woq and Tek to where Ochri's spirit had come from, when it came from the east ahead of Okat.

Okat's third shape was still difficult to find, because when Okat left her hiding place and became a panther, she immediately covered over the scent at her hiding place with panther urine. Tek and Woq cast right past the pungent patch of urine several times, until at last Woq thought to paw aside the urine–soaked leaf litter and soil.

There at long last they found the end of a small, nearly invisible tunnel, hidden under a rock, where Tek's more sensitive nose detected the light and delicate scent of chipmunk, infused with the scent of Okat.

Chipmunks were usually very good at keeping their scent away from their tunnel entrances. But Okat, while waiting in her chipmunk shape for Ani's child to be born, had spent far too much time at her tunnel's entrance, checking the air for scents.

The knat's four shapeshifters now understood why Okat had been able to leave and enter the knat without being detected: chipmunks dig very long and deep tunnels, always with several different entrances. There were many places inside the knat where the entrance to a chipmunk's tunnel could easily be hidden. And there were many more places outside the knat where an entrance would blend in perfectly.

The four shapeshifters tried to find all the tunnel entrances, both inside and outside of the knat's walls. They found only one inside the knat, and another outside it. They blocked them both, but knew there were bound to be others.

They revised their nightly watch, pairing bird with four–legged surveillance, the better to detect Okat going through the knat as a small darting chipmunk. Tsihi and Woq took the first half of each night; S'Kaw and Tek took the second half. Woqri's spirit usually followed either Woq or Tek, trailing them in case they missed something.

They came to know the norms of the knat's nights so well that the slightest anomalies stood out all the more.

Meanwhile, Tek's new dreams were changing, though they did not get more persistent. The hare dream became the most frequent one, and as the hare darted erratically in its flight the predator seemed to anticipate its direction better, and close the gap faster. At the end of these dreams, right before the predator was about to get the hare, Tek felt he could feel the predator's breath on the hare's fur. Upon waking abruptly at that point, the hare's heartbeat echoed in his mind while his own heart pounded with the hare's fear.

A different type of dream began around the same time. In it the prey animal — usually a hare — suddenly turned into the same type of animal as the predator that was chasing it, and the two predators fought tooth to tooth, claw to claw. It was all very odd and confusing.

Tek felt no especial urge to go to the forest, either as buck or to see if he could shape shift into the new shape. Perhaps the urge was lessened by his changing into a buck every night for his part of the watch, alert for any sight, sound or scent that disturbed the stillness of the knat at its rest.

* * *

For a moon and a half after the birth of his son, Roh was besotted with everything about the infant. He raptly announced new developments almost daily, to anyone who would listen. A seminal moment came when he learned with absolute certainty that his son knew his father's face apart from all others.

Roh had brought two men with him to the bench outside his living compartment, where Ani sat holding their son. As the three men stood before the mother and infant, the infant's gaze fixed on Roh and he gurgled and smiled at him. The men with Roh hid their boredom while Roh enthused overlong about this new proof of how smart and wonderful his little son was.

But the weather got colder and harsher, and the irritations of being packed in a crowded clanhouse in the dead of winter inevitably compounded one another. Nearly everyone became snappish and unpleasant. Roh's fascination with his son waned enough for him to long for the refreshment of a brisk winter hunt. He practiced his bowing and readied his gear for an upcoming hunt.

The knat was large enough to have three groups of winter hunters. On average each group had seven short notches on the time stick — one long notch[10] — between hunts, and were out on the hunt for about fourteen short notches — two long notches.[11] At any given time two groups were out, while the third group was resting up and readying itself to leave. When Roh was ready, he let it be known that he would join the next group that went out.

He was surprised when the shaman sent for him and in private tried to dissuade him from going. The shaman did not give him a clear, specific reason to stay home. Instead, he spoke oddly, hesitantly of weird, dark shapeshifting dreams and such, as if the shapeshifting stories he'd been telling lately had spilled over into his dreams.

This was the second time the shaman had told Roh what he should do. The first had been when he advised Roh to stay with Okat, instead of leaving her to live with Ani. Roh had not followed that advice, and as a result he was far happier than he had ever been. He had not known how good his life could be, until he left Okat. Those thoughts strongly influenced him as he weighed whether or not to follow the shaman's advice this second time.

---

[10] one week
[11] two weeks

Roh also felt that the shaman was getting too old and doddering to be a good shaman. He stumbled more of late, and sometimes his words were garbled and vague. And Roh disliked the shaman's musty old shapeshifter stories, and all the nonsensical shapeshifter talk that the stories generated.

Thus Roh made his choice, to ignore the shaman's counsel once again. He was touched though, when the shaman came to him the evening before he left on the hunt, and gave him an amulet to take with him, to ward off evil. It was a rather nicely rendered head of the Good Twin, carved from bone. Roh liked it so much, he looped a strip of deer sinew around its top knot and tied it to his belt.

That group of hunters left the knat not long after the Snow Moon[12] began, on a trip that everyone hoped would not be very long.

A new snowfall came a few days into their trip, followed by a brutal cold spell. Then the Snow Moon began to live up to its name: every day for five days snow fell in great, deep pelts, until in some places the settled snow was nearly as high as a man's chest.

It was during the first of these daily snows that Roh lost the amulet that the shaman had given to him. The hunters had found some moose tracks; while they were trying to follow them in the falling snow Roh noticed the amulet was gone. His knot must have worked loose, or the length of sinew had broken. Roh felt an odd sense of dread when he discovered that the amulet was missing, and thought about re–tracing his steps to try to find it. But he stayed on the trail of the moose with the other hunters until the snowfall's accumulation hid it from them. By then it was far too late to go back to look for the amulet.

In the successive days of deepening snow all game and their snow trails seemed to disappear from the forest. The hunters sloughed along on their snowshoes until they reached one of their remote camp shelters. They holed up there to wait for the snow to stop and for new game trails to appear. Roh along with the others resigned himself to endure the wait. Stored up recollections of his wife and treasured son comforted him when he was awake. But when he slept, terrible dreams plagued him, dreams of his precious child

---

[12] February, usually.

slaughtered by a wild animal in the forest, while his distraught wife ran and cried in the snow.

The dreams became so persistent and realistic that Roh became frantic to return to the knat. To explain his edginess and to try to dissipate the power of the dreams, he told the others about them. At first, they tried to talk away the worst implications of his dreams, and calm his fears. But eventually they agreed to go back as soon as they possibly could.

Chapter 15

Okat knew that her former husband Roh had left the knat in a hunting party. She had been monitoring the trail that the hunters always used at the start of each winter hunt. Further on they would take any one of several trails through the forest, but the first trail was always the same. She simply waited downwind of this trail, in a place where she could scent, and also see, if her husband was among the hunters as they passed by.

The day that she saw him it was so cold that scent did not travel nearly as well as usual. She only caught his scent after she saw him go by. When his scent did reach her and lingered on her palate, Okat kept herself still, remembering the day in the preceding summer when all she had done to get him and to keep him as her husband, had come to naught. All the work of ensnaring him, of catering to his every whim to please him — he destroyed it all on that day when he stood before her and her mother, and told them that the marriage was over, and that he had already removed his belongings from the clanhouse.

Now at long last, the time had come for her to show him the enormity of the mistake he had made on that day.

She turned and went in the direction of the knat, stopping along the way only to fill her belly, by hunting and killing as a panther.

As she neared the knat she proceeded very cautiously. She stayed downwind and did not get close to the knat until a snowfall began. Long before the snow ended at about two hands deep, she arrived at a large tree that was downwind of the knat. She climbed the tree as a bear and then shapeshifted through to chipmunk, to reach an abandoned squirrel's nest, lodged high in the tree's branches. There she made herself cozy to watch and wait.

After the snowfall it got colder. Okat stayed in the tree nest for several days as a chipmunk, observing the late return of one of the other groups of hunters. The hunters only had one slain deer with them, and part of another. Game was scarce and hard to find in falling snow.

Apart from the hunters' return, Okat observed little activity outside of the knat walls. Boys and a few men came out, but because of the extreme cold they did not stay out long. They brought water from the spring, fished on the river ice, or made quick checks of their snares for small game.

The boy Tek was among those who fished. Watching him, Okat thought of how she was going to enjoy catching him alone in the forest, someday soon. She would savor killing him, and perhaps also eat his heart and liver if she happened to be hungry enough.

A few times she saw Woq slip off into the forest and was tempted to follow him and kill him. But she stuck with her purpose in coming here. Both of their deaths were less important to her and could wait, as could the demise of the two bird shapeshifters. All in due time.

The air then warmed enough for more snowfall, and the first of what promised to be several snow storms left a new layer of soft snow everywhere, another two hands deep. It began in the night and ended mid–day. Okat could not see over the knat walls because of the rise that the knat was on, but she knew what the people inside were doing. They were clearing paths everywhere, trampling some of the snow down and shoving the rest of it along the sides of the clanhouses and the knat walls. Outside the knat, the only trodden paths were light ones to the spring and the river. Anyone wanting to go anywhere else had to go on snowshoes.

Late in the night after that storm ended, Okat left the tree and approached the knat in her panther shape, with utmost stealth. Another snowfall had begun; there was no almost no moon and the sky was low with heavy clouds. Each paw was so carefully placed that her movement did not disturb the silence. She was a mere, faint shadow falling on deep pristine snow.

The entrance to the first tunnel that Okat went to was blocked, but the second was undisturbed. As chipmunk she went through the long underground passageway into the knat, where the main branch of the tunnel came up into her family's clanhouse, next to one of the posts where her living compartment had been for so long. She slipped outside the clanhouse's bark wall and scrambled up between the wall and packed snow, until she could see, listen and smell in the air outside of the clanhouse.

All was very quiet and still. And there was only one clanhouse between where she was and the clanhouse where Ani lived with the child.

She readied herself for her flit across the first path but paused to assess a slight sound. Buck scent wafted toward her, so she waited. Tek as buck turned a corner and went silently down the first path she would be crossing.

As always when one of those she had plans to kill was so tantalizingly close, Okat felt a strong impulse to surge after Tek and bring him down with her panther teeth and claws. But with cold calculation she checked the impulse. She had waited long for what she sought this night, and this skinny buck boy was a lesser prey. It was only his close proximity that tempted her so sorely away from her purpose.

She let him go past and when he rounded the next corner she dashed across the path, scrambled between the snow and bark wall, and slipped inside to cross the clanhouse's interior width.

*   *   *

Tek paused, not sure whether there had been a disturbance behind him. The noise he thought he heard had been so brief and slight — hardly more than an eddy of air. He turned back to check it. When he went back around the corner, he saw Woqri's spirit coming toward him between the two clanhouses. As he watched her, she pointed emphatically and mimed a small creature running between them. Tek immediately gave two short, abrupt snorts — quiet but loud enough to alert S'Kaw. He went to the place indicated by Woqri's spirit and began to cast for scent.

But Okat was already across the path on the other side of the clanhouse, and was scrambling between the snow and wall of the clanhouse where Ani lived. Inside she moved rapidly to the center hall. She shapeshifted through woman to bear and located Ani's living compartment almost immediately by scent. Then as a woman she stoked the nearby fire enough to revive its embers into a low

119

flame. If the light or her slight noises woke anyone now it didn't matter: she had plenty of time for what she was going to do.

There were always tallow–filled shells by the fire pits. Okat lit the reed piece in one and took it with her into Ani's living compartment. The baby was propped up near Ani, wrapped and tied to its board. As Okat expected, some of Roh's weapons were on a nearby shelf — he had always left them so when he had been her husband. She grabbed one of his knives and plunged it deftly into the infant's neck with one hand, while at the same time roughly shaking and kicking Ani awake.

Ani woke, groggy and confused. She was not sure whether she was dreaming, but her first thought was to check her baby.

There was light in the compartment and someone's naked back was between her and the baby — there was a woman crouching over her son. The woman turned her head toward Ani, and Ani saw that the woman's face was horribly disfigured around one of the eyes. It took Ani only a few seconds longer to realize that the naked woman was Okat.

Okat's lips twisted into a cruel smile, and she thrust something into Ani's hands. It was a knife that was wet and slippery with a dark substance. Ani looked at the shadowy knife trying to comprehend — a heartbeat later she hurled herself past Okat to protect her infant boy. But it was much too late to save him. He was dead, his neck nearly severed by a deep bloody cut. And Okat was gone; to Ani she seemed to have simply disappeared. But she was at that moment a rushing chipmunk, nearly out of the clanhouse.

Outside a hawk's shrill call sounded, waking Woq and Tsihi and many others. Before the call died away Ani's hysterical cries began.

* * *

After Tek as buck had signaled to S'Kaw, he cast about in swirling snow to find Okat's scent. Upon finding it he raised his head, not certain what to do. Woqri's spirit came through the clanhouse wall, gesturing for him to go around it.

Woqri's spirit followed him; on the other side of the clanhouse he found the scent again, and followed it to the wall of the clanhouse that Ani lived in. Woqri disappeared through the wall of that clanhouse.

120

Tek was feeling odd; it was a little like being in a waking dream of hunting the chipmunk as small prey, instead of, in reality, scenting for it as a buck. He had a strange desire to catch the chipmunk for food.

Suddenly S'Kaw swooped down. Woqri's spirit joined them, coming through the clanhouse's wall. She looked horrified and was clutching her neck. S'Kaw instantly emitted a shrill hawk call; moments later came the frantic shrieks of Ani from inside the clanhouse.

S'Kaw shapeshifted to woman to tell Tek to watch for Okat at one end of the clanhouse; she would watch at the other; Woqri's spirit was asked to watch where they were then. S'Kaw shapeshifted back to hawk on her way to her position above the clanhouse's main door. She was nearly there when Okat as chipmunk darted out from under the main door and rapidly shifted through woman to panther. S'Kaw let out another signaling shriek; she needed Woq to help her but he was not there yet.

*   *   *

When Okat heard S'Kaw's first hawk call, she decided to slip through the knat as panther until she reached the tunnel entrance she had arrived from — she would be safer and faster as panther. And if anyone got in her way, she would kill them.

Okat heard S'Kaw's second hawk call above and behind her but did not pause. She turned toward her destination and saw Tek as buck at the far end of the path alongside the clanhouse where Ani's wails, and a confusion of shouts and cries, could be heard. The buck was coming toward her in the falling snow, and it was alone, other than some faint, wispy girl spirit. Even with the hawk nearby, the buck boy was so enticingly vulnerable. It would take such a short time to kill or at least maul him. In an instant Okat changed course and charged toward the buck.

Woq was running and Tsihi was fluttering toward the noise of the distraught clanhouse when they saw the panther charging toward the buck, with the hawk wheeling for a dive.

The panther was too close to Tek for him to run. He raised his front hooves, but that did not daunt the panther — it was so easy for a panther to evade a deer's hooves.

121

In the last moment before the panther reached Tek, Woqri's spirit threw herself at the panther's head and good eye. Okat as panther barely felt the spirit's meddling, but it made her miss the buck's neck. Instead of her teeth sinking into his neck, she found herself shaving past it. No matter; she twisted, and grabbed with her claws and teeth to flip herself onto his back instead.

Tek as buck twisted and lashed out with his front legs as the panther slipped to one side of him. But instead of seeing his flailing legs and hooves in front of him, Tek momentarily saw his hands, and then the front paws of a lynx in their place. Reflexively those paws grabbed at the passing panther, which Tek knew was going to twist around toward his neck. Tek as lynx twisted around faster and scrambled madly onto the panther's back, trying for the neck but instead sinking his teeth into a shoulder.

The panther, which was three times Tek's size and weight in his lynx shape, shook his hold loose and attacked him. The panther's teeth closed on his neck but he managed to twist and tear with all his might at the panther's chest and belly.

Tsihi as owl rose and then dived toward the fray talons first, opening her wings near the end of her dive to direct her talons at the panther's good eye. But the hawk overtook her in flight, and the hawk's beak snapped the radial bone in one of her wings. She spiraled down and away. Woq caught her, and quickly handed her off to his sister.

Awakened knaters had gathered, some of them armed. In the fitful torchlight, Woq shouted that the panther was Okat, and that another shapeshifter was fighting her as a lynx. The shaman took up his shouts, as did his three siblings who knew the shapeshifting secret.

The hawk landed beside Woq and shifted rapidly to S'Kaw and then through to lynx, bigger and darker than Tek's lynx, though still much smaller than Okat as panther. Hesitating only a moment to gage her best spring at Okat's head and neck, S'Kaw threw herself into the rolling writhing mass that was Okat and Tek, as they bit and ripped at each other on the ground. But Okat, sensing S'Kaw's attack, twisted violently, and S'Kaw did not get as good a hold on Okat as she needed. The panther rolled over the smaller lynx to fight the larger, stronger one. The smaller lynx squirmed free of the panther and in moments the three of them were a blur of snarling biting and tearing fury. Blood and torn fur flew from shredded flesh and deep punctures. Even Woq, who had shifted to wolf and was looking for an opening to join in the fight, could not tell them apart.

Suddenly a momentary balance of grasp and bite among the three cats slowed their spinning, churning mass. Woqri's spirit dropped onto them to hold the moment a little longer, and Woq located the panther's head in the melee by its disfigured eye. He sprang for the head and got one of his bottom fangs through the panther's good eye while his top fangs latched deep under the panther's jaw on the other side of its head.

Woq was rolled under and then up and over, as he held on with his jaw locked. Whenever in the chaotic struggle he found something to brace against he pulled and yanked with his strong neck muscles to sink his teeth ever deeper into the eye and jaw edge of the panther. The panther's blood began to pump into his mouth. Woq yanked with his most powerful jerks to increase the gushing out of the panther's lifeblood.

The movement of the gruesome mass of battling animals slowed. With an enormous surge the panther broke free of it, but did not go far. Snarling, fully blind, it staggered waywardly while the last of its lifeblood throbbed down its chest and bloodied the snow. Soon afterward it fell over. As it took its last ragged breaths, to the accompaniment of anguished moans and cries coming from Ani in the clanhouse nearby, it shapeshifted for the last time, back into its birth shape, into the woman Okat.

While most of the knaters stared through the snowfall at the lacerated woman lying on the ground where the panther had been, Tsihi, Sho and Woq's family rushed to where the two lynxes lay on the ground. Woq as wolf stood there panting, his mouth dripping Okat's blood. He saw his sister Woqri's spirit hovering over the larger lynx's body on the ground. He and those who had joined him watched as the lynx shapeshifted back into S'Kaw for the last time, as she died.

Tsihi knelt beside S'Kaw's body with her husband Sho. Her left arm hung bloodied and useless by her side. Her grandmother had snapped her wing to save her life, and the life of her unborn child, by forcing her out of the fierce battle with Okat. The injury was permanent. Tsihi would have limited use of that arm for the rest of her life, and would never fly again.

* * *

Sho had known for a long time that his wife Tsihi and her grandmother S'Kaw were bird shapeshifters, but he had not known the rest, even about his brother Tek, until a short time ago. He had woken to the shrieks and cries; he grabbed his weapons, lit a pine knot and rushed out of the clanhouse toward the noise, calling and searching for Tsihi. When he got to where the commotion was, Woq's sister thrust his wife into his hands, as a small owl with its bloodied wing. Tsihi shifted from owl to woman in his arms. She gabled some frantic words and tried to rush into the swirl of fighting animals, but Sho would not let her go. He pulled her away from the sight of it and told her again and again, until at last she heeded him, that she had to calm herself for the sake of their unborn child. She calmed enough to tell him that the small lynx was his brother Tek. He asked about the larger lynx and she stilled, and told him that lynx was one of her grandmother's shapes.

Tsihi had not seen her grandmother shapeshift to lynx. She had thought that she was there somewhere as hawk. Tsihi now told Sho that S'Kaw almost never used her lynx shape. Lynx was so contrary to hawks. And to owls.

Sho held Tsihi's head to his chest, and watched the fray for them both with increasing dread. Even after Woq sprang into the fight as wolf, Sho saw how the unequal battle was probably going to end for the two lynxes.

The moment the panther broke away from the other animals, Sho and Tsihi hurried over with Woq's family to Woq and the two lynxes. As they watched, the larger lynx turned back into S'Kaw as she died, while the smaller one — his brother Tek — simply . . . disappeared. One moment he was there, and in the next there was no trace of him at all, except for his blood in the snow where he had fallen.

The night was nearly spent. Throughout all of the night a light snow had been falling off and on. As the day began the snow fell more blindingly. To some in the knat, it seemed as if the snow was

124

trying to bury the knat under a massive pelt of cleanliness, of forgetfulness.

But, of course, the knat could not be so easily cleaned, and what had happened was something that could never be forgotten.

* * *

In the morning the shaman visited each clanhouse, to tell everyone, outright, about the shapeshifters in their midst.

He began with the clanhouse of Ani's family. There he listened to Ani's disconnected pewlings about a naked woman, a disfigured eye, and Okat being there and thrusting the bloody knife into her hands. The shaman assured the clanhouse that Ani had not killed her own child with the knife. Instead, he explained how it had been done by Okat, and about the other shapeshifters of the knat.

When the shaman went to the S'Kaw clanhouse, those in it who did not already know of its shapeshifters were enlightened.

Woq went with the shaman to the clanhouse of Okat's family. Many of that clanhouse had seen Okat change from panther to woman at her death. The shaman told them the rest of Okat's shapeshifter secret. To reinforce the truth of it, Woq turned to wolf before their eyes, circled their main fire, with hackles raised, and then turned back into a man.

Gravely the shaman explained that Okat had long ago killed the girl Woqri, and more recently as panther, she had killed their own clan mother Ochri, and the girl Oji. Some of the women of the family wailed or wept as he spoke of Ochri's and Oji's bravery, and of how Oji had blinded one of Okat's eyes. Some of the men showed an impotent anger against Okat. The loss of their loved ones was so recent and painful.

The shaman went on to tell them that Okat had killed Ani's infant, and was responsible for the deaths of clan mother S'Kaw and the boy Tek. Even though the boy's body was gone, it was clear to everyone who had seen him lying on the ground as lynx that he could not have survived his wounds.

The great, proud clanhouse struggled to accept that the deaths of so many innocents had been caused by their clanswoman — that such a wanton killer had been spawned and nurtured in their midst. They had known that Okat had never loved as the rest of them

125

loved. But they had never expected her to act so much against the honor and standing of their clan.

As the shaman made his rounds, he was asked why they had not been told of the shapeshifters sooner. Most of his listeners knew the answer before he replied. The shapeshifter secret was a sacred one, shared only in extremity. And though the shaman and the other shapeshifters had feared the worst from Okat, they had never known for certain what further lengths she would go to. It was always easier to see where a path was after it had been travelled, than before.

When at length the shaman was done, the knat fully understood Okat's evil, and it derived some grim comfort from its recollection of her still, bloodied body lying in the snow.

* * *

Throughout the snowy day the knat prepared the three bodies for their journey, and began again the rites of mourning.

The infant's body was lovingly cleaned and wrapped for its journey. For the last time, it was carefully tied to its board with gentle fingers.

S'Kaw's body was dressed in its ceremonial clan mother robes and wrapped for its journey with love and respect.

Okat's body was wrapped for its journey by her own clanhouse, declining the assistance of any other. Its actions and its mourning were scrupulous, but perfunctory. The rites were performed adequately, but with abhorrence, and without any trace of affection or love.

Chapter 16

That night S'Kaw's spirit visited each of the clanhouses. In her ceremonial clan mother robes, she stood before the main entrance of each one. At most of them there was only the night's silence. But her spirit tried to commune with each of them all the same.

In life she had always been on alert and calculating the best course for her clanhouse and, by extension, her knat. She had struck forcefully, or nurtured brusquely, or stood by, depending upon the dictates of her long sight. Now in death she was freed from having to avidly watch, and calculate, and choose each course. That heavy mantle was thrown off.

Before the doorway of most of the other clanhouses, she gave her thanks for the many years of shared nurturing, and of striving together for the common good of the knat. She offered what peace she could for the slights and disagreements, most of them seeming unimportant now. She left counsel, hanging in the air, for the wellbeing of those who deserved it. She left her view of a fitting justice for those who did not.

Even though most of the clan mothers were not conscious of her visit, they all awoke in the morning feeling a deeper, wiser mourning for her.

At the clanhouse of Ani's family, S'Kaw's spirit listened for a while to Ani's inconsolable moans and cries. The young woman did try to contain her grief for the sake of her clanhouse's rest, but her misery continually burst from her all the same.

It was snowing when S'Kaw's spirit reached the clanhouse of Woq's family. Woq as wolf sat at the main door. Sitting beside him was his clan mother, wrapped in a large warm bear pelt. His sister Woqri's spirit was there as well.

Woq had told his clan mother that S'Kaw's spirit would come in the night. When it arrived, Woq stood and put one of his paws on his clan mother's lap. This was the signal to her that S'Kaw's spirit was there. She sat up on her knees and inclined her head in the direction that Woq was looking. She spoke quietly to the spirit. She thanked S'Kaw for her great sacrifice for the sake of them all. She pledged that her clanhouse would seek to be very close with S'Kaw's, and would always try to watch over it and care for it, more than ever before. Woq later told her that when she finished speaking, S'Kaw's spirit bowed her assent and thanks.

Woq shifted to being a man so that he could ask S'Kaw's spirit a question. Woq first told the spirit that Tek had disappeared at the end of the fight, leaving no scent to show where he had gone. He asked S'Kaw's spirit if she knew whether Tek still lived somehow, somewhere. He asked her to show her answer by nodding or shaking her head. He shifted back to wolf to see the answer given by the spirit.

S'Kaw's spirit looked long at Woq. For the rest of his life Woq remembered the sharp, dark gaze of the eyes, the impenetrable calculations going on behind them. But the spirit then slowly shook its head.

When S'Kaw's spirit went to the clanhouse of Okat's family there was only silence.

S'Kaw's spirit went to her own clanhouse last of all. Tsihi as owl waited in front of it, with Sho by her side. S'Kaw's spirit approached and knelt in a sitting position before them. The spirit looked at Tsihi searchingly, not certain whether Tsihi truly understood that it had been necessary to maim her, in order to save her life, and the life of her child. Tsihi bobbed her head and shapeshifted to woman to speak to her grandmother's spirit. She assured her grandmother that she *did* understand, and that she honored her grandmother for what she had done. She spoke her grief and sadness, telling her grandmother that she would miss her terribly.

Tsihi asked one question — the same question that Woq had asked, and received the same answer.

* * *

Day came. In the morning the death circle was walked for the infant and for S'Kaw together. They were then taken together to a special place on a rise of ground where their bodies were to be burned on a large pyre, in a place cleared of snow. It was a beautiful spot in all seasons, not far from a creek that ran in a shallow cut through the area.

Okat's family kept apart, mourning as well but understanding the feelings of the others.

Out of respect for S'Kaw's part in killing the murderer of their infant, Ani's family wanted the infant to be placed on the chest of S'Kaw's wrapped body, within the reach of her spirit's sheltering arms. This was done, and their bodies were consumed by the flames together.

In the afternoon the death circle was walked for Okat, by all except Ani. After the morning's exertions, Ani was raving. Her clan mother grimly walked the circle twice; once for herself and once as Ani's proxy. Everyone walked the circle with eyes cast down, with thoughts very private. No tears were shed, except for Okat's victims. Afterward the proper rites were observed, but with no feeling of regret for Okat's death. Okat's pyre was lit in an inferior spot that was often flooded by the river. In choosing that spot it was hoped that the flooding would take Okat's evil away from them and dissipate it. The pyre was large enough to send her spirit on its way, but no larger. All of the appropriate rites were performed, but the only words in them that were heartfelt were the ones exhorting Okat's spirit to be on its way and leave them in peace.

During the ten days of mourning Tsihi rarely left her clanhouse, but Woq often roamed the knat at night, as wolf. The first time he saw a fragment of Okat's spirit in the knat, he tensed to spring at it, elusive though it was. But it was followed very closely by S'Kaw's spirit carrying the infant, and by Woqri's spirit. S'Kaw and Woqri's spirits constantly harried Okat's, giving it no rest. Woq saw them all a few more times, and then he saw only S'Kaw's spirit with the infant, and Woqri's spirit. After the tenth–day ceremony he never saw any of them again. He liked to think that Woqri's spirit made its journey west at last, accompanied by S'Kaw's and the infant's.

He never saw Tek's spirit, either in the knat or in the forest when he visited the places that he knew were Tek's favorites. At times he felt as if Tek was right beside him, and he thought he even scented him then. But it was all illusory. When he turned to look there was never anything there, and when he sniffed carefully he never found any fresh scent of Tek.

* * *

On the day before the ten–day mourning ended, the hunting party that included Roh returned to the knat. They had left their camp and headed directly for the knat as soon as the heavy snows ended. They travelled as quickly as they could, but even with their snowshoes enlarged it was rough and slow going. Near the end of their journey back they came across a fresh deer trail and followed it, floundering, until they caught up with the deer and shot an arrow through the exhausted animal at close range. Though they were all famished, they didn't stop to eat any of the meat. They gutted and poled their kill, and labored through the snow with it to the knat, a meager showing for all of the effort and misery of their trip.

When they got close to the knat a boy out checking his snares saw them, but instead of coming over to greet them, he turned and hurried back to the knat. The hunters made their way over to the snowshoe path the boy had already made in the snow, and followed it in.

The wiser among them recognized that the boy's behavior was ominous. They were certain that some bad news awaited them at the knat. Their thoughts turned to Roh's wild dreams and his fears for his infant. Uneasily they remembered the wild panther screams on the night of the infant's birth, and the horrible death by panther that had been suffered by both Ochri and Oji.

Roh also had these dark thoughts but he forced them aside. He was in the lead, straining every fiber of his being to reach his precious child and wife.

When they were nearly there and on a trodden path, the shaman came out of the knat and stood in front of the entranceway, waiting for them. A few others stood behind him, including the chief.

But before the returning hunters reached where the shaman was, Ani rushed out and raced toward them, barefoot and nearly naked, wild eyed, keening and babbling incoherently. Women from her clanhouse hurried after her, but they were not able to catch up with her.

130

Roh knew the instant he saw Ani that their child was dead. He moved forward numbly to take her into his arms, but the moment they touched Ani changed from a miserable, wildly pleading creature into a completely mad one. She scratched and bit and screamed at him as only the insane can do. It took several of the men to pull her off him. As they carried her back to the knat, she twisted and contorted in their grasp, screaming in primal agony.

She was taken back to her clanhouse and tied to a rack that already had been used twice to restrain her in the days following the death of her child. She had only been off the rack for one day since the second time, when her husband's return precipitated her return to it.

Once Ani was tied down the women of her family took over and did their best to soothe her. Over many days they talked quietly and kindly to her, choosing what they spoke of with great care. They were boundlessly attentive and patient with her, and the men did their part as well, including by taking the children out of the clanhouse with them as much as possible. For a very long time, the noise of children was kept from Ani's hearing as much as possible.

If Ani had been left to heal herself among the more brusque, less loving of the People, she probably would have never healed. She would have either wasted away, or walked uncaring into the forest one day, never to return. But the clanhouse of her birth — though it was not known for having the most athletic prowess, or for being among the wisest — it was acknowledged to be one of the knat's most compassionate. It also had a scrappy toughness: it had determined to save Ani's ailing, fragile mind if it could, even though that was not what Ani herself wanted. It had tallied up the wrongs that Okat had done to the clanhouse, and resolved that Ani's mind was not going to be among Okat's horrific scalps, if there was anything they could do to prevent it.

Even so it took a long time to bring Ani to a better, quieter state, with moments of lucidity. And it took a much longer time for Ani to consistently desire to live her life again.

Roh reluctantly followed the women's advice to keep away from her until they determined that she could tolerate his presence in short, well–timed stints. He spent much of his time away from the knat, on hunts, on trips to other knats, or just alone in the forest to

131

quiet his grieving heart by himself. But he always returned to Ani and to her clanhouse, which cared about him in his grief, as it had in the better days before the great tragedy of his life.

Eventually Ani and Roh were able to live together and support each other again. They had several children and raised them lovingly. But their sorrow over the loss of their first child, their innocent infant son, always shadowed their lives.

Chapter 17

Near the end of the Bud Moon[13] Tsihi gave birth to her first
child, a beautiful, healthy girl. And for countless generations
afterward, the first–born girl also had a girl as her first child.

Tsihi never developed any shapes other than owl, nor did Woq
ever develop a shape other than wolf. They only rarely showed
themselves as such in the knat; they agreed to do so only when they
judged, after serious consideration, that the hearing and night vision
of an owl, or the keen senses of a wolf, were essential to forestall
some grave harm to the knat.

Woq eventually married and had children. Later still he became
shaman, as did many in his maternal lineage after him. Woq himself
was acknowledged to be one of the knat's greatest shamans,
renowned for his sagacity — though in private, there was grumbling
that he was ever prone to talk overmuch.

Okat's family made what amends it could for Okat's killings of
the girl Woqri, Ani's infant son, clan mother S'Kaw, and the boy Tek.
It scrupulously included Tek in the blood debt because the boy was
never seen nor heard of again, and they accepted the shaman's
assurance that he probably would never be able to return. The blood
debt was paid over many years by giving a deference to the
preferences of the three victimized clanhouses — a deference that
Okat's family would otherwise have been unlikely to bestow. They
were a strong, proud family that consistently produced the greatest
hunters and warriors of the knat. They rarely felt that another
clanhouse knew better or deserved more than they did. But when
called upon, they paid off some of the debt each time, until

---

[13] April, usually

eventually it was paid in full, several generations past the lives of Tsihi, Sho and Woq, though they all lived very long lives.

A number of times this unwilling deference kept the Ochwah knat from the brink of war with other knats. But it wasn't long after the blood debt was paid, that a great war broke out, and the Ochwah knat was swept into it. It lost many of its men in the war. But the knat itself managed to survive, and on the whole, it continued to maintain an important place for itself among the People, for many more generations.

End of Book One

~ *Note to the Reader* ~

Tek's story does *not* end here. It continues in Book Two, <u>Nika Rising</u>.

Afterword

This fantasy book and its two sequels were inspired by the indigenous cultures and myths of the northeastern forests, in what is now the United States of America. The three books do not adhere rigidly to documentary sources, but in my 'flights of fancy', I've tried to retain the *essence* of those cultures and myths.

You will not find the panther wind's daughter among the indigenous myths. She is my own creation, but she is of the same *ilk* as existing myths that explain powerful forces in nature.[14]

Whenever little is actually known about prehistoric culture, I've tried to be plausible. For instance, with respect to the disposition of the dead by the northeastern indigenous, some sources refer to low mound burials, others to placing the wrapped body in a tree or on an overhead platform; a few refer to cremation. I chose cremation as a credible practice for an area with frozen, snowbound land during a substantial part of each year.

I'd also like to mention that all of the personal names and a few other words — such as knat — are made up. Why? I did not want to use names and words associated with *specific* indigenous groups. Remember: this story is a fantasy, and it begins in prehistoric times, providing latitude for these innovations.

---

[14] There are many fine books on indigenous myths. My recommendation for 'beginners' would be <u>American Indian Myths and Legends</u>, selected and edited by Richard Erdoes and Alfonso Ortiz, Pantheon Books, 1984.